BACK TO BOLOGNA

MICHAEL DIBDIN

Back to Bologna

faber and faber

First published in 2005
by Faber and Faber Limited
3 Queen Square London WC1N 3AU

Typeset by Faber and Faber Limited
Printed in England by Mackays of Chatham, plc

A CIP record for this book
is available from the British Library

ISBN 0–571–227759

2 4 6 8 10 9 7 5 3 1

To Kathrine

'Someone should kill him.'

Bruno didn't reply.

'Well, I don't actually mean that, of course,' Nando went on.

'Not literally.'

'No.'

'As in a knife through the heart.'

'For example.'

'You were speaking allegorically.'

'Er . . . yes.'

'My client's intention in allegedly uttering the phrase "Someone should kill him" was entirely euphemistic, not to say parabolic.'

'Right. It's just that if the smarmy bastard should happen to drop dead . . .'

'Which God forbid.'

'. . . then that would solve all our problems.'

'Says who? The next one could be even worse.'

'Worse than Curti? You must be joking.'

'Plus you're assuming that anyone in his right mind would be prepared to buy a club where half the players are on a loan or time-share deal with other teams, and the rest will be sold off at the end of the season to meet the budgetary shortfall. It would take years, not to mention very deep pockets, to turn *i rossoblù* around.'

'All right, so hold the heart attack, cancel the stroke. Now what? One more season like this and I'll . . .'

Nando broke off as the car's headlights picked out an amazing pair of black legs displayed up to the white silk triangle of the crotch.

'Keep your eyes on the road,' Bruno grunted sourly.

'Get stuffed.'

'By her? Any time.'

'Or him.'

'With legs like that, who cares? God, I'm bored.'

Nando turned the radio back up.

'. . . created several good chances, particularly in the second half, but this merely served to underline the thing that Bologna fans have been talking about all season, and in all honesty for many seasons past, namely the lack of a world-class striker who could capitalise on the many opportunities going to waste out there and put the ball in the net. The service from the wings and the midfield is always reliable and occasionally inspired, but when it comes to finishing it's the same sad story week after week . . .'

Bruno yawned massively.

'So how are the kids?' he asked, cutting the volume of the radio to a plaintive whine.

'All doing well except Carmelo. He's got some sort of canker on his ribs just below the wing. It must be bothering him because he keeps gnawing at it.'

'Can't you put some sort of bandage on it? Or just tie him up till it heals?'

They drove past a rare prominence in this two-dimensional landscape, one of the vast tumuli where the city's garbage was interred, its burning vapours a perpetual flame of remembrance.

'They go crazy if you try and restrain them. I'm taking him to the doctor tomorrow. He needs to get on a course of antibiotics.'

'They say now you shouldn't overdo that stuff. Lowers your immunity to flu or something.'

'Birds don't get flu.'

'Sure they do. Remember that Chinese chicken scare?'

'Carmelo isn't a chicken.'

Nando was a handsome hunk from some village down in the Abruzzi that Bruno had never heard of, whose latest doomed dream was to get his hands on the ten-cylinder, 500 bhp, 300 km/h Gallardo coupé which the Lamborghini company had recently donated to the Polizia di Stato for mutual public relations purposes. Built like a wrestler, with a neat black beard and an amiable but unfocused smile, he had for some reason married himself off to a skinny, neurotic harridan from Ferrara. Presumably to compensate for the fact that their marriage was and would remain childless, the couple kept a total of eleven parrots and cockatoos in their two-bedroom apartment. The birds perched on your shoulder, nibbled your ear and shat on your jacket, and the whole place stank. Bruno had been there for dinner. Once.

He and Nando were on their way back to headquarters after having been called to the scene of an alleged burglary out in Villanova. The complainant was a slyly pugnacious electrical contractor whose wife had just left him and gone home to live with her mother, taking their six-year-old son with her. He claimed to have come home after work to find the apartment gutted of just about everything except the plumbed-in washing machine. Since the sophisticated alarm system that he had himself installed had failed to respond, then clearly his estranged spouse, the only other person who knew the deactivation code, must be the guilty party.

It had taken over three hours to take the man's statement and to question his neighbours, none of whom had noticed anything amiss. Bruno more than half suspected that the electrician had cleaned the place out himself over a period of several days, put the stuff in storage under a false name, and was now making a formal *denuncia* to back up an insurance claim and ensure that the 'thankless bitch' who had made his life hell got a fair ration in return. As far as the police were concerned, it would almost certainly be a total waste of time, demanding wads of completed forms, written reports and lengthy communication with the authorities in Ferrara, and never getting anywhere.

Bruno didn't care, even though being rostered that night had meant missing Bologna FC's local derby at Ancona, postponed from shortly before Christmas after the original fixture was cancelled due to a pitch invasion. He was bored and hungry and tired and looking forward to going off shift as soon as they got back to the Questura, but at a deeper level he was still blissed out, even though months had elapsed since the miracle had occurred to cut short his 'hardship posting' in the far north of the country and bring him back to Bologna. The young patrolman had stopped going to mass when he left home, but he had recently paid several visits to San Domenico, his neighbourhood church, and on each occasion had set ten euros worth of votary tapers burning before an image of the saint in a chapel where they still provided real sweet-smelling beeswax candles, not the moulded plastic electric bulbs that were replacing them these days and which always reminded Bruno of an amusement arcade. Maybe it had even been fifteen euros the first time. Anyway, at least he'd paid for them, unlike some people, hence the coin-in-the-slot replicas.

On a rational level, of course, he knew precisely how his early return from the German-speaking Südtirol region had come about, but this didn't alter the fact that a miracle of some sort had definitely been involved. Consider the odds. First, this high-flyer from the Criminalpol squad in Rome named Aurelio Zen gets sent up to Bolzano on some shady case with important political ramifications the exact nature of which Bruno had never understood. Second, he, Bruno, is detailed to drive the ministerial envoy or whatever he was to a windswept inn on a God-forsaken pass way up in the mountains on a back road to Cortina. Third, Bruno himself – stuck in said inn for the rest of the day while his passenger goes off with a young Austrian witness to pursue his investigations – finally cracks up under the dour cloud of graceless silence and the glares of loathing lasered his way by the locals, and finally freaks out completely at a café where he and Zen stop on the way back down the mountain, screaming actionably offensive abuse at the stocky, stolid Teutonic blockheads who have made his life and those of all his fellow recruits a misery for months on end. Fourth, instead of putting him on a charge for grossly inappropriate behaviour such as to cause serious unrest in an area notorious for its political sensitivities and separatist aspirations, this Vice-Questore Zen offers, without even being asked, to try and have Bruno transferred back to Bologna immediately, despite the fact that his posting still had over three months to run. Fifth, and most unlikely of all, his benefactor delivers. Was that a miracle, or what?

The two patrolmen were taking the shortest way back into the city centre, along the state highway that parallels the A14 autostrada from Ancona and the Adriatic coast, looping through the unlovely dormitory suburbs to the north of Bologna to connect with the spinal cord of the A1. There was little traffic about, so when a huge eighteen-wheeler overtook them aggressively by running the orange signal at an intersection it made quite a statement.

'Let's take that cocksucker,' Nando said, reaching for the siren and lights.

Bruno laid a hand on his arm.

'Calm down. There's some German name on the front end and the trailer has Greek plates. Probably on his way north from Bari out of his mind on amphetamines, pulled off the

5

autostrada to have his personal needs attended to by a col-
league of that young lovely we spotted back there. Okay, he
was blatantly disrespecting us, but do you really want to spend
hours of overtime this evening finding an interpreter, phoning
whichever consulate is involved, and then dealing with the
lawyer his firm will hire, not to mention the mountains of
paperwork? We've had enough aggravation for one day.'

'All right, all right!'

Nando sounded peeved.

'You're right about Curti, though,' Bruno added in a conciliatory tone.

'That stinking *parmigiano*! As far as he's concerned,
Bologna's just another glitzy status toy like his yachts and his
whores and his villa in Costa Rica. The only thing he couldn't
buy was his hometown club. Sorry, Lorenzino, Parma FC is
not for sale. No problem, he just jumps in his Mercedes, drives
a few exits south on the A1 and buys the red-and-blues
instead. But he doesn't give a damn about us!'

'You're right. The fans could forgive almost anything else,
but there's no sense of passion, no deep commitment.'

'Above all, no money.'

Bruno yawned again, staring sightlessly at the neat rows of
identical six-storey apartment blocks now sliding past the car
like packaged goods on a conveyor belt.

'Well, he's got problems in that department.'

'How do you mean?'

'This tax scandal.'

'Tough. Why should he pull the club down with him? And
now they say that half the sponsors are going to pull out to
avoid the risk of being tainted if the case ever comes to court.'

'Which it won't.'

'Of course not, but that doesn't help us. The damage has
already been done. We're just . . .'

It was then that they saw the car parked at the roadside, its emergency blinkers flashing. Nando braked hard, swerving sharply to the right in a controlled skid, and pulled up behind it.

'Blow job,' he said.

'Or breakdown,' Bruno replied. 'I'll go and check.'

He stepped out into the freezing February night. For some reason, the cold seemed colder here than it had in Bolzano, harder and seemingly obdurate. Maybe it was the humidity seeping down from the Po delta, he thought, or more likely the pollution. Average winter temperatures were a good ten degrees lower up north, but there the air was bone-dry and crystal clear. Still, spring would soon be here, and he was home. That was all that mattered.

The illegally parked vehicle was a blue Audi A8 luxury saloon. Bruno automatically noted down the licence number. That was about all he could make out in the glare from the patrol car's headlights behind. The headrests on the front seats made it impossible to see whether there was anyone in the car. Bruno walked round to the passenger side and peered in through the window, then rapped sharply on the glass. There seemed to be a man sitting in the driving seat, but he did not respond and the door was locked.

Bruno was about to return to the patrol car for a torch when the full beams of a van coming in the other direction bathed the interior of the Audi in light. The illumination lasted only a few moments, but it was enough. The driver of the Audi was sitting quite still. The expression on his face suggested that he was struggling to achieve some trivial but impossible task, like drawing out the plosive 'p' into a long dying murmur.

Bruno stepped away from the car and called in on his radio. He spoke little but listened intently, shielding his left ear against the roar of traffic on the banked and cambered curve of the motorway above. When he returned to the patrol car, his face was blank.

'It's not a Merc,' he said, slamming the door shut and shivering.

Nando looked at him askance.

'I know, it's an Audi. So what?'

'That conversation we just had?'

'About Curti?'

Bruno did not look at him, just sat staring ahead at the blue Audi saloon.

'Just don't mention it, that's all. When they get here.'

'When who gets here?'

Bruno slammed his open palm loudly on the dashboard.

'We never discussed the matter, all right? We don't give a shit about football.'

'But that's all I do give a shit about! That and my birds. Oh, and Wanda, of course.'

'That a new purchase?'

'Wanda's my wife!'

'Oh, right.'

Right! Worked as a PA for some lawyer downtown. Nando did not deign to reply. A heavy silence fell.

'That car is registered in Lorenzo Curti's name,' Bruno remarked quietly. 'There's a man sitting in the driving seat. It's hard to tell in this light, but he looks quite a bit like the photographs and TV footage I've seen of Curti. Quite tall, slim, a well-trained beard, salt-and-pepper hair.'

'Did you talk to him? Why did he stop?'

Bruno opened the window a fraction and cocked his head as though listening.

'You know those knives they use for splitting blocks of Parmesan cheese? Well, they're not really knives, more like triangular chisels. Thick, sharp and very rigid.'

'For fuck's sake, Bruno, you're starting to sound like that singing chef on TV. What have Parmesan knives to do with anything?'

'The man in that car has what looks like one of them sticking out of his chest. As in a knife through the heart.'

Through the opened window, a loud and rapid chopping sound asserted itself in the distance. Bruno opened the door.

'Help me get the flares out and clear a space where the helicopter can land.'

At about the time that the blue Audi A8 – covered in a tarpaulin, with the driver's body still behind the wheel – was being winched on to a low-loader for transport to the police garage, Aurelio Zen and his phantom double were deep underground somewhere in the wilds of Tuscany.

It had been a long day, a long month, indeed a long life, thought Zen. Or maybe it was his double who had these thoughts. It had never been established whether he could think, but the question was of no real importance. The essential point was that unlike Zen, whom he outwardly resembled in every last detail, he had no feelings. Perhaps this explained why he looked so disgustingly hale and hearty. There might be a few silver tints in the lustrous black hair, a heightened tautness of skin over bone here and there, but these merely added to his general air of distinction and maturity. Here, one felt, was a man who had lived and learned much, and now, in full command of this accumulated experience, was in charge of his life like an accomplished horseman of his mount, not striving fretfully to dominate and control, but serenely conscious of and responsive to every eventuality.

It was difficult not to envy such a man, although he showed no more hint of possessing any sense of superiority than the Matterhorn – or indeed of having any feelings at all. To Zen, who nowadays seemed to have, and indeed to be, nothing but feelings, this was in itself supremely enviable. Whether physical (throbs, tingles, twinges) or mental (despondency, dizziness, dread), feelings had so intensely taken over his consciousness as to banish even the memory of other perspectives. He had once been someone else. That much seemed probable, although it could not of course be verified. The fact that he no longer was that person, on the other hand, was irrefutable. All the personal qualities, opinions, skills, ideas, habits, likes and dislikes, together with similar data subsumed by the words 'I' and 'me' – in short, everything about Zen, except for his feelings – had apparently been transferred as though by electronic download to the *Doppelgänger* currently visible beyond the darkened carriage window. As for the discarded husk and its prospects for the future, the less said the better.

It had to be admitted that the specialist whom Zen had gone to Rome to consult had viewed matters rather differently.

'A good recovery,' had been his verdict after inspecting the X-rays, inserting a monocular catheter like some giant tropical worm down Zen's oesophagus, and vigorously kneading the flesh around the surgical wound as if intending to barbecue it later.

'But I feel terrible,' Zen had murmured in response.

'Are you in pain?'

'It's not so bad now. But I feel totally exhausted all the time. The slightest effort, and I have to lie down for half an hour to recover. Walking up a flight of stairs leaves me breathless and dizzy. Even talking drains me.'

His voice dispersed like smoke.

'That's to be expected,' the consultant replied with heartless nonchalance. 'Your system is still healing. That leaves it less disposable energy for other tasks.'

'I know, but there's more to it than that. I just don't feel myself any more. I don't feel like me. And perhaps I'm not.'

The consultant closed Zen's file with a flourish, then tapped the cover several times as though to emphasise the profession- al significance of this gesture.

'Medically speaking, as I have already explained, the prospects for a full recovery are excellent. The duration of that process depends upon too many variables to quantify with any precision.'

He glanced pointedly at the clock, his interest in the case clearly at an end. Like a policeman who knows there is nothing more he can usefully do, thought Zen. In the past, he too had often made it brutally clear that he had no time to waste, but now any such attempt would ring hollow. The plain fact of the matter was that time to waste was all he did have.

Perhaps the consultant had allowed himself to be touched by the expression on his patient's face, or perhaps he was more subtle than Zen had given him credit for. At all events, as they shook hands at the door, he asked an unexpected question.

'Is your wife being supportive?'

Zen did not answer for so long that the silence finally became embarrassing. First he had to work out that his 'wife' must be a reference to Gemma, who had made the appointment for him at a time when he had felt too weak to deal with hard-bitten Roman personal assistants with an attitude as long as their credit card statements. As for the query itself, that seemed unanswerable. The story was far too long and complex to sum up in a few words. It would take hours to explain even the bare outlines of the situation.

'Supportive?' he managed at last.

The consultant clearly wished that he had never spoken.

'Oh, just generally,' he said dismissively. 'You've got to remember that the whole business must have been disturbing for her too. In fact it's often harder for family members than for the patient, oddly enough.'

Zen thought, but no words came.

'She's been . . .' he began, and broke off.

The consultant nodded with transparently fake enthusiasm, murmured 'Good, good!' and walked quickly away.

One feature of Zen's condition that he had not bothered

mentioning was that bits of his body he had never used to think about now demanded his constant attention, while others, on which he had unconsciously depended, were now conspicuous by their absence. It thus came as no particular surprise that the dull roar in his ears suddenly receded to a distant murmur, while the shrilling of his mobile phone a moment later sounded perfectly normal. He studied the strip of transparent plastic where the incoming call was identified for the length of five rings before answering.

'I'm on the train. We were in a tunnel.'

'How did it go?'

It took Zen some time to answer.

'It was a normal tunnel,' he said at last. 'Perhaps a bit longer than most.'

'Tell me what the doctor said.'

'I just did.'

'Are you feeling all right?'

'The doctor says I'm fine. It's just that I'm in a long tunnel.'

'But there's light at the end of it?'

'No, it's dark now. It must be there too, surely.'

A sound like some cushions make when sat upon.

'What time do you get in?'

'I don't know.'

'Do you want me to pick you up? I was thinking of going to a movie.'

'Go, go! I'll take a cab. Or walk.'

'What about dinner?'

'I had a huge lunch and I'm not hungry. Go to your movie. I'll let myself in and . . .'

He broke off, realising from the increased background noise and air pressure that the train was sheathed in yet another tunnel, cutting off the conversation between him and Signora Santini.

Not that it took much to do that these days. The cut-offs, drop-outs, robotic acoustics, phantom voices and dead silences in their communications were becoming more frequent all the time, as if the entire network had gone bust and was being progressively run down. He could have sworn that her very voice – the voice he had fallen in love with on the beach in Versilia that memorable summer – had become harder and more strident, appending an unspoken 'take it or leave it' edge to the most commonplace remark. And he sensed that authentic anger, concealed like the raw hurt of his own mangled bowels, lay just below the surface of quotidian banality, securely rooted and feeding, for the moment, on itself. In short, the affectionate, calm and dependable woman he had fallen in love with had grown distant, capricious and tetchy. So it seemed, at least, but Zen accepted that he was the least reliable of witnesses. A stranger to himself, what could he know of others?

The earlier mention of food pushed him out of his seat and along the carriage, grabbing at each seat-back to keep his balance, precarious everywhere these days. In the buffet car he bought a plastic-wrapped ham roll and a can of beer and carried them over to an elbow-high ledge by one of the windows, where his double was already installed. Maybe she had met someone else when he was in hospital. Or indeed before, during the period when he had been away on his last case. Or before that. It wasn't unlikely. Both partners are always at least subliminally aware of the balance of power in their relationship, and the fact was that Gemma was younger than him and still very beautiful. Moreover, he knew that she had enjoyed a certain reputation for flightiness before they got together.

He munched his way ravenously through the roll, having lied to Gemma about his 'huge' lunch. In his present state, Zen could only achieve anything by breaking the task down into small, achievable subsets and then concentrating wholly on performing them, to the exclusion of all else. Today his chosen assignment had been to get to the consultant in Rome in time for his appointment. He had accomplished this, but at the price of forgetting totally about other matters, such as making an appearance at the Ministry and possibly seeing his friend Gilberto. He had even forgotten to eat. There were times when he remembered his period in the clinic almost with nostalgia. Everything had been so simple then. No one expected you to be competent or to take any initiatives. On the contrary, such behaviour was frowned upon. The staff told you what to do and when to do it, and you obeyed them. There was no need to plan or act. In retrospect, it had all been very relaxing.

He finished the rather dry roll, washing it down with the rest of the beer. To be honest, he realised, the visit to the consultant had been just a pretext. His real reason for going had simply been to go, to escape the encircling walls of Lucca. This massive brick barrier had once seemed reassuring, but after one month bedridden and another confined to the apartment in Via del Fosso, it had become as spiritually suffocating as it literally became in high summer, shutting out every open perspective and refreshing breeze. No doubt that was why he had arrived in Rome hours before his appointment, killing the time by sitting around in cafés and gazing mindlessly at everyone who came and went, like a tourist. And afterwards, instead of taking the first train north, he wasted further hours at a cinema in a seat so close to the screen that the movie was an incomprehensible blur. Now, though, he was on his way home, this brief spell of parole at an end. It could be prolonged slightly by deliberately missing the connection at Florence, so that by the time he arrived back at the apartment, Gemma would with any luck be asleep.

But there was still tomorrow, and the day after, and all the days after that. Once upon a time he could have turned to his

15

work for distraction, but it seemed doubtful, feeling the way he did, that he would even be able to hold down the sort of routine administrative job he had been allocated years before during a period when he was in disfavour, doing the rounds of provincial headquarters to check that the petty pilfering and misappropriation of funds were being kept within broadly acceptable limits. In a word, his career was over. He had been granted indefinite sick leave once the extent of his medical problems became clear, and the temptation now was to string that out for as long as possible, then parlay it into early retirement. He had a powerful backer at the Ministry, and was clearly of no use to anyone. A gilt handshake seemed to offer the most painless solution to this embarrassing situation for everyone concerned, and he could see no reason why it should be refused.

Which left the question of his personal life. Zen had had relationships go wrong before, of course, and had felt amazed, dismayed and at a loss, but this time the effect was much more intense, perhaps because the possibility of its happening had never occurred to him. Neither Zen nor Gemma had bothered to get a divorce from their previous partners, and so the question of their remarrying had never arisen. But to all intents and purposes they had acted, and had seemed to feel, as if they were indeed husband and wife. More often now, though, they resembled two boxers circling each other warily, occasionally jabbing out, then getting into a clinch and pounding each other at close quarters with no referee to pull them apart. There was never any winner, only two losers, and the contest invariably ended with Gemma stalking out and slamming the door behind her.

Turning to the window, Zen eyed his spectral other, so smugly solid and substantial. He felt as if he were the reflection and that image the original. 'A shadow of his former self,' as the stock phrase went. A hopeless invalid. A sad case. The long, sleek train poured out of the final tunnel and clattered over the bridge across the Arno. In the past, on his weekly visits to the Ministry, Zen had always felt a lifting of the heart at this moment, because it was when he felt that he was almost home. Now, for exactly the same reason, it filled him with foreboding.

When Vincenzo burst in, Rodolfo was lying naked on the bed and savouring one of those rare moments when, to quote a German poet recently cited by Professor Ugo, 'a happiness falls'. What had he done to deserve this? The answer appeared to be nothing. At the advanced age of twenty-three, Rodolfo was reluctantly coming to terms with the fact that he was not one of life's natural achievers, a doer of deeds, attainer of goals and winner of women. If he had won Flavia, for the moment at least, it was only because she had fallen into his hands. There was nothing wrong with his intellect, but when it came to everything else, he seemed to be an under-motivated if well-meaning lightweight who had always taken, and no doubt always would take, the path of least resistance.

A happiness had fallen, and he had been fortunate enough to be there to catch it, but you couldn't count on such luck indefinitely. Normally what fell broke, or broke you if you were standing unawares beneath. Rodolfo's father had continually striven to remind his son of such basic facts, in a weary but dutiful tone of voice which suggested – indeed, almost proudly advertised – that while he had accepted the utter futility of any such attempt, he would not have it said of him that he had shirked his paternal responsibilities.

The thought of his father had brought to mind, by natural degrees of progression, the family home, the little market town, and the whole intimately immanent landscape of his youth. Puglia! So when Vincenzo burst in, resembling an Errol Flynn lookalike after a particularly hard night's carousing, his flatmate felt naked in more ways than one.

'*Siamo in due,*' he hissed angrily, yanking the covers up over Flavia's torso and his own genitals.

The intruder leant on the door frame like a drunk against a lamppost.

'Where the fuck's my fucking jacket, you cunt?'

As always, Rodolfo marvelled at how repulsively attractive Vincenzo was, with his sleek black hair, aquiline features, intense eyes, slim body and devastating devil-may-care manner.

'Jacket?' he replied, getting out of bed and pulling on his jeans.

'My football jacket! It's disappeared!'

Vincenzo grasped the shapeless, acid-green polyester garment that he was wearing over an incongruously fashionable dress shirt.

'I had to borrow this piece of shit from Michele. I want my own jacket to go to games in, God damn it! My signature jacket!'

Rodolfo steered his flatmate out into the living room and softly closed the bedroom door behind them.

'You mean the black leather one with the Bologna FC crest on the back?'

'Of course I do! I've worn it to every single match since . . . For years and years. For ever! It's the team's lucky charm! When I don't wear it we lose, just like we did tonight.'

Rodolfo gestured apologetically.

'I'm sorry, Vincenzo. My coat was stolen at the university. I haven't been well, as you know, and it's freezing cold out there so I borrowed one of your jackets. You weren't around, so I couldn't ask, I just took the shabbiest one I could find. I didn't realise it was so precious to you. You've got tons of clothes, after all.'

Vincenzo Amadori's extensive and eclectic wardrobe was indeed one of the principal reasons why he and Rodolfo were sharing this relatively luxurious apartment in the first place.

'I'm really sorry,' Rodolfo repeated. 'Your jacket's safe next door, but I don't want to turn the light on and wake Flavia.'

But Vincenzo, typically, had already lost interest in the subject.

'Who cares?' he said, dismissively waving a limp hand. 'It's all hopeless anyway.'

'We lost?'

'We lost. But it doesn't matter.'

'How come there was a game tonight? It's midweek.'

'Postponed from the original fixture. Cancelled due to a spot of nastiness engineered by yours truly. So we all had to go back to Ancona. The fans, the player, the manager, the owner . . .'

'And we lost.'

Vincenzo roused himself briefly, felt in various pockets and finally produced a bottle of *limoncello*.

'Leading at half-time and then pissed it away, with a little help from the ref as usual. Three-one final.'

'You just got back?' Rodolfo remarked, to get off the subject of the match before Vincenzo started insulting him as a shitbrained southerner, a Bari supporter whose sister did it with Albanians. It was just a matter of time before Vincenzo twigged that Flavia was from the unfashionable side of the Adriatic and made some remark which Rodolfo would not be able to overlook.

'Shit happened,' his flatmate replied with that raffish smile he could switch on and off at will. 'I was out of it, Rodolfo. Way, way out!'

He took a long, gargling swig of the lemon liqueur. Rodolfo noted that it was the genuine pricey product made exclusively with fruit from the officially guaranteed zones in Capri and Sorrento. Nothing but the best for Vincenzo, even when his goal was oblivion.

'Well, I'm glad you got back all right,' he said, making a show of concern before returning to the bedroom and Flavia.

Vincenzo again smiled the raffish smile that he could switch on and off at will.

'Somebody gave me a lift. And then . . .'

He broke off, clutching his stomach, then tried unsuccessfully to stand up. Familiar with these symptoms, and mindful of the fact that he would have to clean up any resulting mess, Rodolfo went to help him.

'And then?' he prompted, trying to keep Vincenzo's brain engaged and his reflexes dormant.

Vincenzo shook his head urgently and plunged down the hall to the bathroom. A moment later came loud groans followed by the sounds of repeated vomiting. Rodolfo sighed and returned to bed, locking the door behind him.

'I don't like your friend,' said a quiet voice.

'He's not my friend. We share this apartment, that's all.'

Flavia edged herself upright in the bed on each elbow alternately, the fleece of dark-red hair tumbling over her shoulders and breasts. She cleared it off her face, lay back on the pillow and reached for the pack of cigarettes on the bedside table.

'Why?' she asked.

As so often, out of sheer ignorance of the basic logic of the language, she had wrong-footed him. That was what happened if you had affairs with foreigners, Rodolfo reflected sourly. Next thing you'd be falling in love and deciding that their banal gaffes were actually profound insights into the human condition.

'Why what?' he asked irritably, his idyll now completely disrupted. He was equally angry with Vincenzo for waking Flavia, and with Flavia for allowing herself to be woken.

'Why do you share with him?'

Rodolfo lay down on the bed beside her.

'I don't know. It just happened. Like you and me.'

Flavia smoked quietly and made no reply, her startling blue eyes regarding him with no little concern.

'I got back after Christmas to find that there'd been a fire in the building where I had been living,' Rodolfo went on. 'It was a question of finding alternative accommodation, and fast. On the allowance my father gives me I didn't have a lot of choice, and of course most places were already let for the whole academic year. So I photocopied some ads with those tear-off strips and pinned them up all over the university district, but nothing came of that. Then someone who was moving out of this apartment tipped me off about it. It was out of my price range, but I came round to take a look anyway and ran into Vincenzo as I was leaving. He'd heard about the place independently, and of course money's no problem for him. He paid the landlord a deposit right away and then suggested that we go and have a drink together as he had a proposition to put to me. I didn't know him, but he seemed pleasant enough. Anyway, classes had already started and I couldn't afford to be choosy. Over coffee – well, he had something stronger – he suggested that since there were two bedrooms we should share the apartment and split the rent. When I told him that even half would be a stretch for me, he said, "All right, you pay a third, on condition that I get the big bedroom. I don't care about the money, but I need my space and I don't like living alone." So there you are. Pure chance.'

'There's no such thing as chance.'

Rodolfo laughed.

'If you kept up with the news, you'd know that there's nothing else.'

The girl frowned.

'So you're not – what is it? – *credente*?'

'A believer? Of course. I'm a fervent Protestant.'

'Really?'

'Absolutely. I protest against everything.'

Flavia's frown deepened.

'I try to watch the news, but I can't always understand.'

He leaned over and kissed her pale face.

'I don't mean the small screen, I mean the big picture. And there's nothing to understand. Or better, nothing that can be understood. Deterministic materialism is the only game left in town. The intellectual high rollers have figured out the odds down to the last decimal point, and basically they agree with Vincenzo. Details aside, the deal is that shit happens.'

From the hallway, as if on cue, came the sound of the toilet flushing. There followed various unidentifiable thumps and bumps, and finally the slam of the other bedroom door.

'Yes,' said Flavia.

'Yes what?'

'Yes, I understand. But . . .'

She fell silent.

'What?' Rodolfo insisted.

But Flavia shook her head in that decisive way she had.

'Never mind,' she said. 'It's none of my business anyway. What do I know about this country, what's normal and what's not? I'm just passing through. Another piece of shit working its way through the system.'

Rodolfo chose to regard this as a challenge.

'Tell me anyway,' he insisted, rolling over and holding her.

'No. It would be *invadente*.'

This gave him a chance to lighten the mood.

'But you are an invader!' he declared, clutching his chest with one hand and flinging the other out dramatically. 'Not only have you invaded my country, but also . . .'

He was about to add 'my heart', but realised just in time that under the circumstances this might not sound like ironic hyperbole but simply hurtful. Lost in her own thoughts, Flavia seemed to pay no attention to the unfinished sentence.

'He reminds me of . . .'

She broke off to shake the ash from her cigarette into the saucer by the bed.

'He's very beautiful,' she finally added inconsequentially.

Again Rodolfo made an attempt at humour.

'Believe me, if I had a single gay gene in my body . . .'

Flavia seemed uninterested in this speculation.

'But he's wicked,' she said, as if pointing out the logical conclusion of her argument.

'What's that supposed to mean?'

Flavia did not seem troubled by either his manner or the question.

'I probably used the wrong word. Or maybe this thing doesn't exist here.'

A radiant smile appeared for a moment, transfiguring her intimidatingly regular features.

'But you spoke of genes in your body,' she continued, expressionless again. 'Well, I have my own genes, and one of them gives me a very clear sense of this thing, whatever you call it.'

She stubbed out her cigarette and lay back.

'Vincenzo's just a spoilt brat,' Rodolfo said in a dismissive undertone. 'Father's a lawyer, mother has a pretend job with the *giunta regionale* fixing up artsy exhibitions and the like. Typical Bolognese upper middle class, in short, with a history of mild political activism when young that makes them socially acceptable now, and enough disposable income to take pricey "alternative" vacations in the Lofoten Islands or wherever. It's all the usual clichés, so Vincenzo's done the clichéd thing and rebelled against the family life he can return to any time he wants. He skips his classes and exams, hangs out with a bunch of low-lifes at the football stadium, and drinks to excess. But evil? He doesn't have the balls to be evil. Or anything else for that matter. The guy's just a wanker.'

Flavia just lay there, gazing up as though at a distant light faintly visible through the ceiling.

'Nevertheless, I know such people,' she said at last. 'Even though I never met them, I know them. Can you understand? Ion Antonescu, Gheorghiu-Dej, Corneliu Codreanu . . . I know them very well.'

Rodolfo yawned. It was late, and he had a lot of revision to do for Ugo's seminar the following day. His attitude to his renowned tutor had become much more overtly confrontational of late, so he'd better be able to demonstrate a flawless grasp of the subject.

'Who are they?' he murmured.

'Which one?'

'Any of them. The last one.'

'Codreanu? King Carol had him killed in 1938. Two years later Antonescu overthrew the monarchy and turned the state into a dictatorship run by the Legion of the Archangel Michael, otherwise known as the Iron Guard.'

Rodolfo yawned again and embraced her.

'You're Scheherazade, spinning me crazy stories to keep me awake all night. You and your Ruritania! I don't believe the place even exists.'

Flavia nodded.

'It's never been very real, particularly if you happened to be a "stateless alien" of Hungarian or Jewish origin. But it does exist. And some of the things that happened there definitely weren't imaginary.'

'Like what?'

It was Flavia's turn to rise, though with evident reluctance, to the perceived challenge.

'Like the sealed rooms. They couldn't afford gas chambers, so they just locked them up and left them to suffocate.'

Rodolfo leaned over her and took a cigarette.

'What's all this got to do with Vincenzo, precisely?' he enquired in the pedantic tone, unwittingly borrowed from Professor Ugo himself, that he employed in the latter's classes.

Flavia took a long time to answer, as though her reply had to travel all the way back from the planet she had been observing earlier, situated at a distance that made even light lame.

'I'm not sure,' she said at last. 'I know only that he is very strong. So am I, but I may not be here to take care of you. And you are not strong, *caro mio*. You're very sweet and intelligent, but you're weak. The man you are living with is none of those things. So be careful.'

Gemma Santini stood in her nightdress, dispassionately surveying the ravages of time in the mirror above the dressing table. Not too bad, all things considered, was her conclusion. Some decorative details might have succumbed to wear and tear, and the odd patch of pediment gone missing, but the Goths and Vandals had yet to lay waste to everything in sight. In short, she still felt reasonably confident that she could get a date, if it should come to that.

Which it very well might, she reflected. This was an uncomfortable thought, but Gemma had never felt at ease with anything but the truth, however inconvenient it might be. Facts had to be faced, whether they were the facts about her own face, as reflected in the bedroom mirror, or about the man in her life, as reflected in the kaleidoscopic sequence of grotesque and disturbing patterns into which their life together had recently disintegrated. Gemma took a modest pride in being a truth-teller who did not spare herself or others; a realist who, whatever mistakes she might make, could recognise them as such and learn to stop making them. And she was beginning to consider her relationship with Aurelio Zen as just such a mistake.

Another characteristic of hers was that having come to this decision – or at least contemplated the possibility of doing so – she had not the slightest interest, unlike her partner, in endlessly analysing the hows, whats, whens and whys of the situation. At the same time she took a certain satisfaction from knowing that if she had chosen to play this game, she could have beaten Zen hollow. There were, for instance, two crucial factors involved of which he remained totally unaware. One he might be forgiven for, since it was a family matter which Gemma had kept from him. He had only himself to blame for his ignorance, however. If you make it abundantly clear that certain concerns of other people are of not the slightest interest to you, it is only to be expected that they will spare you any details of subsequent developments.

The other factor was Zen's hypochondria, in the broadest sense of the term, encompassing not only a morbid anxiety about his health but also chronic depression. Of this, Gemma had originally been as unaware as Zen still was that she herself might be going to become a grandmother. Looking back, she had perhaps been a little slow on the uptake, but then she'd had plenty of reasons for wishing it not to be true. But by now the evidence appeared incontrovertible. First there had been Zen's endless complaints about abdominal pains and a vague sense of lassitude. Then, once it became clear that he had no intention of seeing a doctor of his own free will, Gemma had had to browbeat and virtually strong-arm him into doing so. Diagnosis had proved to be another series of hurdles, involving trips first to the local hospital and then to a private clinic in Rome, where the consultant that Zen was revisiting that day had prescribed a surgical intervention which was reported to have been 'routine and without complications'. The patient, on the other hand, seemed to regard this everyday procedure as a nightmarish and potentially lethal ordeal comparable with being the first-ever recipient of a brain transplant.

And so it had gone on ever since. Like any pharmacist in a culture where, even by strictly legal criteria, the profession is granted considerable discretionary powers, Gemma had her share of regulars who frequently dropped in to discuss their latest ailments and general state of health before asking her to supply 'a little something' to alleviate their symptoms which, however, were 'not worth bothering the doctor with'.

Nevertheless, she had never before encountered a full-blown case of paranoid hypochondria until Zen returned home to recuperate after his discharge from the clinic.

She had initially been indulgent, reasoning that he would soon pull himself together and return to normal. Not only was there still no sign of this, but he seemed to come up with a fresh complaint every day. If it wasn't backache, it was toothache. When those afflictions lost their novelty, he claimed to have terrible migraines that made sleep impossible, so that he felt – there was a lot about his feelings – utterly exhausted, confused and depressed. He couldn't think straight, he couldn't remember anything, and he certainly couldn't go back to his job. He'd finally realised how important his work was to him, and now he would never be able to work again. In short, he no longer recognised himself. 'I just don't feel like me any longer,' he'd moaned. 'It's as if a thread has broken somewhere and the whole fabric is unravelling before my eyes.' These melodramatic displays had finally pushed Gemma's patience to its limits, and the result had been some quite lively rows, followed by long periods of sullen silence. Zen had apparently adopted the tactic of pointedly 'not speaking' to her, which she was only too happy to reciprocate. But things plainly couldn't go on like this much longer.

When the phone rang, she nearly didn't answer it, suspecting that it would be her former lover, as she now thought of him, soliciting a lift from the station, or even from Florence. But the caller turned out to be her son. This was as welcome as it was unusual. It had almost always been Gemma who initiated contact with Stefano, particularly after she had made the mistake of touching ever so lightly on various aspects of his new situation which she privately found worrisome in the extreme. Neither mother nor son had much small talk, but both made a show of chatting briefly about neutral topics such as the weather and Zen's health before Stefano got to the point.

'Actually, Lidia and I were wondering if you could come up here some time.'

'To Bologna?'

'Well, yes. This weekend, if you're free.'

'Has something happened?'

She tried to keep an edge of urgency out of her tone, without complete success. Stefano had obviously been expecting this question.

'We've got lots to tell you, but let's wait till you come. If you're able, that is. But it's hard for us to get away, and . . .'

'Don't be silly! Of course I'll come.'

She replaced the phone with mixed emotions. On the one hand she was looking forward to getting away from her own domestic problems, on the other she was already concerned about those that might await her at the other end. She could think of at least three main possibilities, none of them good. But they would have to be faced anyway, and a change of scenery was a definite bonus.

The echo of a door shutting in the stairwell, followed by a series of trudging, faltering footsteps, warned her that her significant other had returned. She quickly turned off the light, dived into bed, pulled the covers over her face, and was to all appearances deeply asleep by the time that Aurelio Zen hesitantly pushed open the door.

Flanked by two beaming bimbettes wearing smiles as big as their boobs and very little else, Romano Rinaldi grasped the wooden handle of the Parmesan dagger and held it dramatically above his head.

'And now, like an Aztec priest performing the ultimate sacrifice, I open the heart of this cheese, the very heart of Italy!' he cried, plunging the cutter home and simultaneously bursting into a rendering of Verdi's 'Celeste Aida' that went on, and on, and on.

In the soundproofed control booth, Delia's glance met that of the director.

'Coked again,' she muttered.

'You amaze me,' the director replied drily.

He touched a button on the console before him.

'Technical edit,' he said. 'Romano, the teleprompt script to camera three, please.'

He switched off the microphone link to the studio beyond the triple-glazed window.

'I'll cut in some of that promotional footage the producers' association sent us,' he said with a brief, harsh laugh. 'Maybe one of those scenes with lots of cows. Then lay Lo Chef's big aria under, fade it out and meld to the teleprompt VO with cutaways to him gabbing to camera.'

'You're a star, Luciano.'

'Thank God for digital is all. The trailer segment has to be ready to air tomorrow. In the old days, that would have taken Christ knows how many man-hours. Even with the money the *parmigiani* are slipping us under the table, we'd still have had a hard time costing out.'

31

Delia nodded vaguely. She looked, and was, preoccupied.

'How much longer till wrap-up?' she asked.

'Where our Romano's involved, who knows? The studio's booked till noon, just to be on the safe side. As long as he doesn't manage to eviscerate himself with that Parmesan cleaver, we should be finished by then.'

Lo Chef's voice boomed out over the speakers set against the padded wall.

'. . . sixteen litres of the finest, richest, freshest milk to make a single kilo of this, the Jupiter of cheeses lording it over the rabble of minor gods. And then as much as two years of completely natural ageing, according to traditions handed down over seven centuries of continuous production, with no artificial manipulation to influence the process . . .'

Delia walked over and kissed the director lightly on the forehead.

'Do me a favour, Luciano. Keep him at it for at least another fifteen minutes. I'll have to hose him down and mother him when it's over, but I need a coffee first.'

'No problem. If he goes all speedy and rushes through the rest of the script, I'll just tell him he was a bit flat on a couple of bars of that Verdi aria and get him to repeat the whole thing.'

Delia smiled her thanks.

'Hey, did you see that thing that Edgardo Ugo wrote about him in *Il Prospetto*?' Luciano added. 'Got him bang to rights, no? I laughed myself sick!'

Without answering, Delia went out to the corridor. Almost immediately her mobile started to chirp. She checked the screen and said 'Damn!' before answering.

'Have you told him?' the caller asked.

'Not yet,' she replied, ignoring the stairs down to the street. 'He's in one of those moods this morning. You know what he's like when he's taping.'

'Delia, he's going to find out sooner or later, probably within a few hours. The damn magazine is on the streets now. It's essential that he hears the bad news from us. How are you going to spin it?'

Delia pushed open the door to the fire escape, blocking its automatic closing mechanism with her briefcase, and stepped out on to the metal platform.

'More or less as we discussed. The big question is how he'll react. You know how he feels about having his competence called into question.'

'Naturally, since he hasn't got any. But the show is making a fortune for us here at the station, another fortune for Lo Chef and a very nice career for you, my dear. Don't let's screw any of that up just because Romano Rinaldi can't take a joke. And that's all it was meant to be.'

A plane flying low overhead on the final approach into Ciampino put the conversation on hold for some time.

'You're sure about that?' Delia yelled over the final resonant rumbles.

'One hundred per cent. My people checked with Ugo's people today. In any case, none of our audience is going to care less what some professor of semiotics in Bologna thinks. All Romano needs to do is ignore the whole incident and it'll be forgotten in a couple of days.'

Delia checked her watch.

'I've got to go. He'll be off-stage at any moment.'

Actually there were at least five minutes to go, but Delia had never mastered the art of taking a mobile phone call and lighting a cigarette at the same time, and it was the latter rather than a coffee that she desperately needed before bearding her highly-strung client. Unmarried, very ambitious, with a baker's dozen years of ova already addled and a *molto simpatico* but totally ineffective significant other, Delia knew that she couldn't afford to lose this job.

After graduating with a modest degree, she had worked her way up through several jobs in corporate communications and public relations before landing her present position as personal assistant to the celebrity chef whose television show, *Lo Chef Che Canta e Incanta*, regularly pulled in millions of faithful viewers every week. Moreover, the figures were always rising, and there had even been approaches from other European broadcasters interested in acquiring the rights for their own territories. And then this left-wing academic and obscure novelist pops up and lets the cat out of the bag, jokingly or otherwise, thereby threatening to ruin the whole sweet deal.

She tossed her cigarette down into the car park below and went back inside. To her horror, the light mounted above the door to the studio was glowing green. She was late, and Romano Rinaldi didn't like to be kept waiting. She shoved the door open and ran up to the stage where he stood, sweating and hyperventilating, in the toque and white uniform which had had to be changed four times that morning after being spattered with assorted ingredients.

'I'm so sorry, Romano!' Delia said breathlessly. 'I had to pop out for a moment to take a very sensitive business call. I didn't want Leonardo listening in. Actually, it was about something we need to . . .'

'It's nothing,' the star interrupted, jerking both hands outwards as though to symbolise the jettisoning of redundant cargo. 'I don't need any praise or applause. The great artist is always a great critic as well. Today I was magnificent. I know that instinctively, in my belly, in my heart!'

He grasped her arm and broke into the gaping, toothy, beard-framed smile that was one of his professional hallmarks, an image of which featured on the labels for the ever-growing list of sauces, oils, cookware and other products branded under the Lo Chef trademark.

'I'm getting better and better, Delia,' he confided. 'This is only the beginning of the rich, prolific middle period for which I shall always be remembered. The years to come . . .'

Lost for words to describe adequately the splendours of the future that awaited him, he relapsed into a long heartfelt sigh. Delia patted his shoulder.

'I understand, Romano, and I completely agree. Now you go and get changed, and then we must have a brief discussion. I realise that this is a difficult moment for you, after putting on such a superb performance, but there are some very important and urgent issues that we need to address.'

'Yes, yes! Give it to me! Give it to me hot and hard!'

King Antonio perched naked on his throne, sweating, groaning, imploring. Then his expression changed to one of alarm, almost of fear.

'Oh my God, it's coming! Ah! Oh! No, I can't! It's too big! It'll tear me apart! Please God, I can't take it!'

At the last moment, just when he knew from the pangs below that he was about to do himself a serious injury, his sphincter relaxed that crucial millimetre or so. After that there were only the gasps, tears and moans, followed by a triumphal flush and the glowing sense of absolute fulfilment.

Next came an invigorating shower, but Tony emerged totally uninvigorated. After a moment's reflection, he swallowed six paracetamol tablets washed down with water gulped from the hand-basin tap. They wouldn't do his liver any good, particularly given his rigid regime of a bottle of bourbon a day, but at least they would ease the vicious headache that had been with him since he awoke.

Straightening up, he caught sight of himself in the mirrored door of the bathroom cabinet. The reflected image was a shock. His forehead was swollen to twice its normal size and, when he touched it, proved very sensitive. Tony immediately thought about malignant cysts, but the thing definitely hadn't been there the day before, so a bruise seemed the more likely solution. The skin was a rainbow in shades of pink, red, purple, blue and black, but didn't seem to be broken.

He walked through to the bedroom, trying to calm down and get the situation into perspective. It was all part of the job, after all. Being the top *investigatore privato* in Bologna was tough work, but somebody had to do it. Still, he wished he could recall a little more clearly what had happened the previous night. He knew that he had fired his current girlfriend, but only because he did that to whoever happened to occupy that position on the last day of each month. Private eyes couldn't have stable, long-term affairs. They were complex, alienated loners who had to walk the mean streets of the big city, men who might be flawed but were neither tarnished nor afraid. Above all, they had to suffer.

Tony Speranza was certainly suffering as he laboriously put on his clothes and went through to the kitchen to make coffee. The resulting brew produced still more suffering, to alleviate which Tony lit an unfiltered Camel, cracked open the Jack Daniels and knocked back a stiff shot. What the hell had happened last night, apart from the screaming match with Ingrid or whatever her name was?

Screaming match. Football match. Of course, he'd been to the stadium to check up on the target's pals. Photograph them at the bar afterwards with that ultra-cool digital camera he'd just bought, barely bigger than a matchbox. It had taken all the experience of the total pro he was to do so without being spotted, but he'd accomplished his mission. Now it was just a matter of downloading the picture files to his desktop and emailing them to *l'avvocato*. Only where was the camera? He checked his overcoat pockets, then patted his suit. His wallet and keys, notebook and pen, were all present and correct. But not the camera. And not . . .

Oh shit, he thought. Oh fuck. Oh my God.

To be honest, Tony didn't really need a gun. Ninety-nine per cent of his work came from divorce cases, jealous husbands, and keeping tabs on the children of local families worried that their costly offspring were getting into bad company and worse habits. *La sicurezza di sapere tutto, sempre!!!* was the slogan he used for his ad in the Yellow Pages and on the fliers stuck under the windscreen wipers of parked cars. The work itself was mostly a question of being equipped with the latest surveillance technology, and occasionally putting in a sleepless night staked out in front of the property where an adulterous liaison or drug party was going on. There was almost never any violence, certainly none involving firearms.

But Tony Speranza knew and respected the rules of the genre. Private eyes have to have a gun, so he had acquired one from a Serbian former special policeman who had done some freelance work for him at one time. It was an M-57 semi-automatic, manufactured to the highest specifications in strictly limited quantities by the Zastava State Arsenal. The pistol fitted unobtrusively into the capacious pockets of the double-breasted trench coat and had a gorgeous walnut grip and silky blued finish into which Tony had had his name engraved in fancy cursive script. A little beauty, in short. The only problem was that he didn't seem to have it any more. 'The assurance of knowing everything, always'. Ha! Right now, Tony would have settled for feeling reasonably sure about anything, once in a while.

This train of thought was derailed by the phone.

'Tony Speranza, *investigatore privato*,' he said automatically.

'This is the office of Avvocato Giulio Amadori,' a female voice stated.

Tony laughed and took a hit of bourbon.

'Hey, I never talked to an office before!'

'Avvocato Amadori wishes to be informed of the current status of the unresolved issues in the matter in which he has employed you.'

'Put him on, darling, put him on.'

'Avvocato Amadori is presently away from his desk.'

'Then let me speak with the desk.'

'It concerns the photographic evidence which you and he have discussed.'

Tony laughed again and lit another Camel.

'You know what? I bet you're not an office at all. You were just kidding around. I see you as a ravishing blonde with a come-hither look that can melt platinum at twenty metres, who knows where all the bodies are buried, and has the murder weapon tucked into her garter belt.'

'To ensure quality service and for your protection, this conversation is being recorded. If Avvocato Amadori considers your attitude inappropriate, he reserves the right to take the necessary steps.'

'Oh yeah? What does he do when he gets mad, run up the bell tower of San Petronio and make like Quasimodo?'

'Thank you. Avvocato Amadori will be informed of your response in due course.'

'Listen, I'm on the job, okay? But discretion is of the essence and so far a suitable opportunity has not presented itself.'

But he was talking to a dead line.

He put the phone down and poured himself another bourbon. I knew the Amadori case would be trouble from the beginning, he fantasised. Of all the PI offices in all the towns in all the world, she walks into mine. In point of hard fact, it was a routine surveillance operation for a fortyish yuppy whose kid had left home and was refusing to communicate with him. Giulio Amadori's main worry seemed to be that Vincenzo would end up in trouble with the cops and that this would reflect badly on his own law practice, although he had made a cursory gesture towards fashionable sentimentality by foregrounding the family reputation and his wife's feelings. He was prepared to pay five hundred up front for details of his son's whereabouts, habits and associates, with the possibility of more to come for follow-up investigations or interventions based on the primary information.

Tony Speranza would much rather have been hired to look into a seemingly casual disappearance that led him to a sexy but dangerous babe with plenty to hide both physically and criminally, but in his experience that sort of thing rarely happened in Bologna. All he had to go on was a snapshot of the young man and the information that he affected to be a diehard supporter of the Bologna football club. Such fans invariably had season tickets at the Curva San Luca end of the ground, and sure enough when Tony headed out to the stadium on Via Costa the evening of the next home fixture he soon identified Vincenzo emerging in a group of his fellow *ultras* from one of the stepped concrete culverts leading down from the stands. He had then followed them through prolonged post-game festivities in various bars and clubs before tailing the target home to an apartment right in the centre of the city.

Thanks to his superb professional skills, Tony had remained unobserved by Vincenzo and his associates on this occasion, but he knew that it would be too risky to repeat the operation regularly enough to provide the total surveillance which his client expected. A remote device was therefore called for, and the question became where to install it. The most convenient location was the target's car, but Tony had already established that Vincenzo didn't own one. The normal alternative was some personal possession or item of clothing in frequent use, and here Tony had better luck.

The Amadori kid spent a lot of time asleep or hanging around the apartment he shared with one Rodolfo Mattioli, a harmless, ineffectual graduate student who didn't appear to socialise with the target. There was also a girl involved, a red-headed stunner that Tony had tracked to her nest and planned to visit in the very near future, but the activities that *l'avvocato* was concerned with invariably involved some or all of the crew of football fans, and when he went out with them Vincenzo equally invariably donned a rough-looking black leather jacket, the back of which was decorated with an oval of shiny metal studs surrounding a painted image of the official club logo and the heading BFC 1909.

The next problem was access. Tony considered various possibilities, but in the end fate handed the solution to him on a plate. The occasion was a home game against the mighty Juventus, for which the Renato Dall'Ara stadium was packed to capacity. In the end Bologna lost to a disputed penalty, so the mood of the emerging fans was far from serene. The police were present in force and made an attempt to direct the *tifosi* of either team away from the stadium separately, but the hard-core elements on either side had had long experience of much more ruthless crowd control than the local authorities, accustomed to keeping a low profile in left-wing Bologna, could bring themselves to impose. Pretty soon those who had come not just to watch the match but to get into a fight managed to drift away down side streets and alleys, reassembling in the car park of a nearby Coop supermarket as soon as the police dispersed. Tony Speranza followed the group that included Vincenzo, keeping a discreet distance and trying to look like an ordinary citizen on his way home.

When they reached the deserted, dimly lit car park, it became apparent that the Juve supporters outnumbered their opponents by about two to one. This advantage increased as some of the *rossoblù* yobs disappeared into the bushes screening off the street, on the pretext of needing to pee, and did not return. It soon became clear that they had made a wise decision. The brawl lasted no more than two minutes, at the end of which the Bologna contingent slunk away to the jeers and laughter of the Torinese. All except Vincenzo Amadori. He stood his ground, hurling obscenities and abuse at his enemies and taunting them to come and get him. This they duly did. Amadori ended up in a foetal crouch on the bare asphalt, where he received a few more vicious kicks before the aggressors tired of the sport and trooped off up the street.

Tony Speranza had been concealed behind a delivery van parked in the far corner of the lot. He now emerged and ran quickly over to Vincenzo Amadori, who was groaning feebly. None of his companions seemed to be coming to his assistance, so Tony unzipped and folded back one side of the leather jacket. The satin lining was quilted in a diamond pattern. Tony took out an Xacto knife and made a small incision in the stitching of one of the diamonds, then inserted the handle of the knife and tore the opening a little more. Into it he slipped an object about the size of a cigarette packet, but as smoothly rounded as a pebble on the seashore and weighing no more. This he positioned in the centre of the padded sac, then pressed both sides hard so that the Velcro wrap would adhere to the fabric. Thirty seconds later he was in a phone box further up Via Costa, summoning an ambulance anonymously to the Coop parking lot. Now the bug was successfully planted, it was in his interests to get Amadori back on his feet and active again as soon as possible.

The device in question was essentially the innards of a mobile phone, stripped of its cumbersome microphone, speaker and other frills, but containing microchips responsive to a number of different networks. Once an hour the unit turned itself on and made contact with the nearest receiver-transmitter mast for each company and then phoned the data in to the computer in Tony's office, where a nifty bit of software translated the resulting triangulation into a time-dated map with a star indicating the position of the target at that moment. Tony was therefore covered if any questions arose about Vincenzo's whereabouts at any particular moment, and without the tedious and potentially tricky chore of actually following the little bastard and his mates around.

So two elements of the assignment had been completed. The third was the set of photographs that he had taken the previous evening, but which had gone missing when he had been mugged and his miniaturised camera and gun stolen. How the hell had that happened? Vincenzo Amadori and his pals certainly hadn't spotted him, Tony reflected as he slipped on the double-breasted trench coat, trilby and aviator shades he had bought online from an American retailer specialising in 1930s retro gear. He would have known instantly if they had. A trained investigator could always tell when he'd been 'made', to use the technical term.

He let himself out of the apartment and walked downstairs to the street. The windscreen of his battered Fiat was dusted with a coating of grey, granular snow from which a parking ticket protruded, one end trapped under the wiper blade. *Comune di Ancona*, it was headed. Below that, in handwriting, appeared the amount of the fine payable within thirty days under penalty of . . . He groaned as the details of the previous evening finally came back to him. Of course! He had indeed been to a football match, only not at the stadium here in Bologna. The fixture, played midweek for some reason, had been an away game with local rivals Ancona, and Tony had duly driven down to that city with a view to completing the photographic record of Vincenzo's cronies.

He started up the car, blotting out the view in a dense pall of exhaust fumes. He had it now, he thought. He'd located the clique he sought, despite the fact that for some reason the target wasn't wearing his leather jacket. After the game he had followed them to a bar and very cautiously taken good-quality shots of the whole group. Mission accomplished, he had then gone to the lavatory at the rear of the bar for a quick pee before heading home.

After that, he had only a confused memory of the door bursting open and someone slamming his head forward against the tiled wall. When he recovered his senses, it had been to find himself on his hands and knees with his face in the trough of the urinal. By the time he had cleaned himself up and returned to the bar, Vincenzo Amadori and his friends were no longer there. Tony had ordered a couple of large whiskies to fortify himself, and must somehow have driven home and got into his apartment before passing out fully clothed on the bed.

In short, he had made one mistake, he thought with some satisfaction as he put the car in gear and backed out of the parking slot. So intent had he been on snapping the circle standing around Vincenzo Amadori without being observed by them that he had overlooked the fact that there were other people in the bar. This wouldn't have mattered in law-abiding Bologna, but Ancona was a port city, crawling with down-and-outs, illegal migrants and criminal elements of every description. One of them must have noted the chic little Nikon nestling in Tony's fingers and determined to make it his own.

He shrugged nonchalantly as he turned right on to the main road into town. All things considered, it was no big deal. He could buy a new camera and didn't really need the gun. Indeed, the lone thief had actually done him a favour. Incidents like that merely validated his status as an authentic *investigatore privato*. Everyone knew that private eyes got sapped all the time. It was part of the job description, particularly if you had to operate in a tough, pitiless part of the world like Emilia-Romagna.

There had always been aspects of life that Aurelio Zen had found problematic, even in the halcyon years before his midlife medical crisis had multiplied their number virtually to infinity. One of them was being brutally woken out of deep sleep, another was talking to total strangers on the phone. The morning following his return from Rome he got both.

He was first bawled and battered into consciousness by a sinister figure in a white hooded robe, who turned out on closer inspection to be Gemma. She had been washing her hair in the shower when the phone rang, and her exertions to rouse Zen caused a secondary shower to splash down on his face, which still bore the traces of a rapidly fading expression of blissful ignorance.

'It's for you!' Gemma shouted, waving the telephone she was holding in one hand while covering the mouthpiece of the receiver with the other. 'Your work! They say it's urgent!'

She emphasised this fact with a kick, which went wide as Zen rolled over in bed at that moment. Gemma promptly lost her balance, dropped the phone in a failed attempt to steady herself, then sat down rather suddenly on the floor. This caused her to swear, and Zen to feel the onset of a rising tide of laughter which soon floated him back to full wakefulness.

As usual these days, Gemma failed to see the lighter side of the situation and flounced out of the room, loudly abusing Zen with a string of vicious expletives and slamming the door so hard that it bounced open again. He went to shut it properly, his initial humour fading fast. What had all that been about? One more irrational and unpredictable fit of hysteria. Welcome to another day at Via del Fosso. The phone lying on the floor seemed to be emitting gurgling sounds. He picked it up.

'*Pronto?*'

'Is this Aurelio Zen?' a voice barked in his ear.

Zen wasted a sarcastically unctuous smile on the plastic mouthpiece.

'It is indeed!' he announced in a falsely jocular tone. 'He himself, as ever was, larger than life and twice as real. And whom, pray, have I the honour of addressing?'

'Gaetano Foschi.'

The name rang a bell, but it was only after the caller had testily supplied further information that Zen linked it with the short-tempered, workaholic southerner who was deputy head of the Criminalpol section of the Interior Ministry.

'What the hell's going on there?' Foschi demanded. 'The place sounds like a madhouse.'

'It often feels like it too.'

'What? Why aren't you answering your duty issue phone?'

'It's not switched on.'

'Why not?'

'I'm on sick leave.'

'Says who?'

'Dottor Brugnoli,' Zen replied with the air of a chess master declaring checkmate.

'Ah, you're one of Brugnoli's babies, are you? Well, I'm sorry to have to inform you that life around here has become rather more spartan during your prolonged absence. As in stake them out on the mountain and see who survives.'

'I don't follow you.'

'Call me back on your encrypted mobile. This line is not secure.'

When Zen did so, Foschi informed him that Brugnoli, Zen's patron at the Ministry had taken up the offer of a consultancy position with a leading bank following a governmental 'crisis' and cabinet reshuffle of which Zen had heard nothing.

'I didn't know,' he explained feebly. 'I had to have an operation and I've been on indefinite sick leave ever since.'

'Very indefinite,' Foschi retorted. 'So much so that there's absolutely no record of the fact in the personnel database.'

'Dottor Brugnoli told me that he would arrange everything.'

Foschi laughed shortly.

'I'm sure he did, but that was before he arranged his own departure to greener pastures in the private sector. Since then we've gone back to playing strictly by the book of rules, according to which you are available for immediate active duty. Are you saying that such is not the case?'

Zen thought for a moment. He could probably get a letter from the consultant excusing him from service for another month or so, and explaining and documenting the record of his case. On the other hand . . .

'What did you have in mind?' he asked.

'It's this Curti business.'

Zen had no idea what he was talking about, but he had already created a bad enough impression for one morning. He decided to bluff.

'What exactly do you want me to do?'

Foschi sighed deeply.

'It's a damn shame you don't live here in Rome like everyone else, Zen. That's something we may have to review in the light of the changed situation. It would make things so much easier if we could discuss this face to face.'

Zen said nothing.

'Anyway,' Foschi went on, 'the Questura in Bologna are handling the actual investigation, but we need someone to go up there and liaise with the Ministry. Your name came up.'

'Why should they tell me anything they don't tell you?'

Instinct told him that bluntness was the best way to whatever organ had been substituted for Foschi's heart.

'They won't. But they'll tell you sooner, and above all you'll be in a position to report back on what they're not telling us.'

'Why should they try and conceal the truth? We're all playing for the same team.'

'I'm not saying that they necessarily will. But they are going to be under enormous pressure to deliver results, and quickly. Lorenzo Curti was a figure of fame and notoriety not just in Emilia-Romagna but on a national and even international level, a millionaire entrepreneur who owned the Bologna football team and was also the majority shareholder in a dairy conglomerate currently under investigation for tax evasion and serious fraud. In short, this promises to be the highest-profile case in the Bologna jurisdiction since the Uno Bianca fiasco.'

After a moment, Zen recalled the spate of serial killings around Bologna in the late 1980s involving a white Fiat Uno. He also recalled that when the perpetrators had finally been brought to justice, they had almost all turned out to be policemen working out of the Bologna Questura, many of them involved in the investigation into their own crimes. It had taken years for morale in the Polizia di Stato to recover from this scandal.

'Forewarned is forearmed,' Foschi concluded. 'Your assignment is not to take command of the investigation but to remain fully informed about progress and to report developments to me personally on a daily basis, and more frequently if necessary. That way, if the media vultures start to circle, we'll be ready for them.'

'I understand.'

'How soon can you get there?'

Zen was about to remind Foschi that he hadn't agreed to go yet, but instantly realised that as far as he was concerned he had.

'In a few hours.'

'Very good. I'll tell them to expect you after lunch.'

When Gemma came in, Zen had already showered and dressed and was busy packing. Without offering a word of apology for the vile names she had called him at their last encounter, she started gathering together her clothes. Clearly this would be another day when they were 'not talking'. Someone else, however, was.

'. . . sure to tune in again next week, when Romano takes a pilgrimage to the temple of the one and only Parmigiano Reggiano!'

'Believe it or believe it not, it takes no fewer than sixteen litres of the finest, richest, freshest milk to make a single kilo of this, the Jupiter of cheeses lording it over the rabble of minor gods. And then as much as two years of completely natural ageing, according to traditions handed down over seven centuries of continuous production . . .'

The television screen at the far end of the living room, visible through the open door, showed contented cows grazing, pails of creamy, pure milk being poured into vats and then cooked in a cauldron over an open fire, while authentic-looking peasants stirred the brew with wooden staves, all interspersed with close-ups of a Luciano Pavarotti lookalike got up in a chef's outfit beaming toothily at the viewer while belting out extracts from Verdi's 'Celeste Aida'.

'Aren't you even going to apologise?' Gemma demanded, pausing in the doorway with her bundle of clothing. As had become customary, she would dress in the spare bedroom. It seemed just a matter of time before one of them started sleeping there.

'I might ask you the same,' Zen replied mildly.

'What have I to apologise for?'

'Ditto.'

'For cruelly mocking me when I fell over! You just lay there cackling instead of even offering to help me up or ask whether I was hurt. And the only reason it happened was because I got out of the shower to wake you for your stupid phone call.'

Zen slipped several strata of socks into a spare corner of the suitcase. He seemed to have only one clean vest. Oh well, he'd buy more in Bologna and then have them washed at the hotel. With the situation the way it was, the last thing he wanted was to raise the question of dirty laundry.

'You're leaving?' Gemma went on, still hovering in the doorway.

Zen nodded. No, not that green horror, he decided. He hadn't worn it for years, but the laws of thrift inculcated by his mother died hard. He laid the rest of the shirts flat on top of the other garments, then closed the case.

'So where are you going to go?'

'Bologna.'

The first flicker of some expression appeared on Gemma's face, but was instantly suppressed.

'Why Bologna?'

Zen was about to tell her, but then decided to let her twist in the wind for a while. It was the least she deserved after the way she'd treated him.

'Years ago I was stationed in the city,' he replied airily. 'I loved it, and I've always wanted to go back.'

Gemma regarded him levelly for some time, then gave a light but studied laugh.

'I could stop you, you know.'

'Really?'

'Well, not stop you leaving. But I could certainly ensure that you enjoy this visit to *La Grassa* a lot less than your last. A single phone call would do it.'

He laughed mirthlessly in turn.

'I doubt that one more of your tirades could ruin my stay. At least I won't be in the same room to listen to it.'

'Oh, the phone call wouldn't be to you.'

Zen set the suitcase on the floor, straightened up and confronted her. She scrunched her face up and narrowed her eyes.

'We have received a phone call, Dottor Zen,' she said in a voice an octave lower than usual and with a passable imitation of the Bolognese accent. 'A Signora Santini, resident in Via del Fosso, Lucca, alleges that just over a year ago you murdered an ex-officer of the Carabinieri, one Roberto Lessi, in her apartment and then forced her at gunpoint to assist you in disposing of the corpse at sea. She further asserts that you subsequently moved into her apartment and have terrorised her both mentally and physically with a view to ensuring her silence. She is prepared to testify to this effect in court. It is therefore my duty to . . .'

They regarded each other in wary silence.

'Bullshit,' remarked Zen finally.

'Don't be too sure. You keep accusing me of acting irrationally. There's no telling what irrational people may do.'

Zen shrugged.

'I've been summoned to Bologna for work, that's all. To be honest, it might not be a bad thing for us to spend a bit of time apart. I've been through a bad patch recently, one way and another, and I'm sure I've been difficult at times. I know you have. Maybe what we need is a cooling-off period to help get things in perspective.'

Gemma's expression softened marginally, but her body remained poised for either fight or flight.

'That time on the boat, Aurelio, when we moored off Gorgona,' she said dreamily. 'Do you remember? You told me then that we were prisoners of each other. Well, that's what I'm starting to feel like. Your prisoner.'

Zen nodded.

'Me too. But perhaps we can both get over it. I hope so.'

He picked up his suitcase. Gemma backed into the living room, keeping her distance from him.

'Do you want me to drive you to the station?'

'No, thank you. I can manage.'

She shook her head sadly.

'No, Aurelio. That's just what you can't do.'

He shrugged this off.

'Well then, I'm going to have to learn.'

'Mattioli, would you remain here?' the professor remarked casually as the rest of the class left the seminar room.

He caught the flash of anxiety in the young man's eyes. He had intended that it should be there. It was part of the charm and style of Edgardo Ugo's post-1968 faded leftist persona that he always addressed his graduate students in the familiar *tu* verbal form, and insisted that they do the same to him. This time, however, he had used the impersonal, distancing *lei*. That, and the use of Rodolfo's surname, made the message quite clear.

'Sit down, please.'

Ugo gathered up his belongings and then proceeded to take some considerable time arranging them in his evidently expensive, but of course artisanal rather than designer, brief case before paying any further attention to the student.

'You're a bright lad, Mattioli, so I'm sure you'll understand that after that last outburst I can no longer admit you to my seminars. There's nothing personal about this. Indeed, I find it painful in many ways. But to do otherwise would be a dereliction of my duty to the other members of the class. They have understood and accepted the principles of the course, and are attending these classes, often at considerable personal or familial financial sacrifice, in the hopes of bettering themselves and making a serious contribution to this academic discipline. They are certainly not here to listen to cheap jokes and mocking asides from someone who, despite his evident intellectual capacities, is at heart nothing but a *farceur*.'

The boy stared back with his unblinking black eyes, as expressionless as the muzzles of a double-barrelled shotgun, but said nothing. Typically southern, thought Ugo. He knows that there's been a war, that he lost, and that there's nothing to talk about. Later he might come round with a knife and cut my throat, but he's not going to humiliate himself further by pointless protests and weak entreaties.

'Should you so wish, you may of course continue to attend my lectures,' Ugo continued. 'Under the rules and regulations of the University of Bologna, you are also entitled to sit your final exams and present a thesis, but to avoid wasting everyone's time I feel obliged to tell you now that I very much doubt whether this would result in your receiving a degree. Besides, the only career possibilities open to a graduate in semiotics are in the academic field. I would naturally be contacted as a referee and I should find it impossible, as a matter of professional principle, to recommend you. I further doubt whether you would prove suited to such a career, in the unlikely event that one were offered you. There are so many talented and excellently qualified applicants these days, and so few vacancies. Quite often the decision comes down to a question of whom the other members of the faculty care to have to meet and deal with on a daily basis, and prickly, rebarbative individuals who like to show off their supposed wit and spirit of independence by making mock of their superiors are, to be honest, rarely anyone's first choice. In short, I suggest that you look into the possibility of an alternative line of study more adapted to your temperament and mentality. Engineering, perhaps. Or dentistry.'

With which he walked out, leaving the young man sitting there in silence. On Via de'Castagnoli Ugo called a taxi, which he directed to his country retreat. His original intention had been to cycle back to the nearby townhouse that he used as a place of refuge during the day and an occasional overnight bolthole, but now he felt an urge to get out of the city. Why this

54

feeling of unease? His decision had been correct and correctly executed, excepting perhaps those last two phrases. But Mattioli had had it coming for some time. The little bastard had been provocative from the very start.

One of Edgardo Ugo's seminarial chestnuts was that, in our post-meaning culture, to move from the sublime to the ridiculous and vice versa no longer required even a single step, merely an alternative selection from an infinite interpretational menu. When he'd brought this line up in the opening seminar of the semester, Rodolfo had replied, 'Excuse me, *professore*. Are you saying that if a recording of the slow movement of Mozart's K364 is being played in the cell where a political prisoner is undergoing torture, his or her resulting experience is simply a function of consumer choice?' Ugo had sensed that Mattioli was trouble right then and there. Knowing the Köchel catalogue number of the Sinfonia Concertante, for example. That was a leaf straight out of Ugo's own book: awe them with your command of arcane documented minutiae, and they'll swallow your big contentious thesis without a murmur.

But today Mattioli had gone too far, not only proclaiming that words had meanings, but that the relationship between language and reality, although labile and demanding constant and close attention, was by its nature (!) both authentic and verifiable. 'The fact remains that there is a real world which exists independently of any possible representation of it, and which in turn conditions any such representation,' he had concluded, with the air of the young Luther nailing his theses to the church door.

Edgardo had handled this arrant nonsense with his usual urbane charm, even getting a round of appreciative laughter from the other students for his learned humour when he suggested sarcastically that to invoke Giambattista Vico's *'sensus communis generis humani'* was hardly *Scienza Nuova* – more

55

laughter – at this late date. Nevertheless, enough was enough. Standards had to be maintained and essential truths upheld. As he had told Rodolfo, it would have been dereliction of duty for him to have acted otherwise. So why did he have this slight sense of uncleanliness, as when you get a bit of meat or spinach stuck between your teeth and can't quite remove it with your tongue?

Twenty minutes later he was back in the spacious landscaping and clear air of his villa, set back from a secluded lane winding through the spine of hills above Monte Donato between the Reno and Sàvena rivers; a mere five kilometres from the city laid out beneath like a map, yet to all intents and purposes another world. For some reason the confrontation with Rodolfo Mattioli was still troubling him, though, so he decided to dismiss it by getting to work.

Two hours passed, and the dusk was curdling beyond the window, before Edgardo laid down his Mont Blanc 4810 Series Limited Edition fountain pen, as thick as a stumpy but fully erect cock, on the sheet of heavy, deckle-edged Fabriano paper, rich in linen and made by hand using methods essentially unchanged since the thirteenth century, then thoughtfully replaced the solid black sculpted cap over its rhodinised 18-carat gold glans. He had chosen these writing tools as appropriate to the task he had just completed, a piece of cheap journalistic fluff designed to promote the recently-released film – very loosely based on a misreading of the superficial plot level of his best-known novel – in some American celebrity gossip rag sold to semi-literate sadsacks at supermarket checkouts.

But as always, the choice had not been easy. Each of the rooms on the upper floor of the villa was a scriptorium, and each quite differently designed and equipped. It was a question of selecting the right one for the assignment in hand, and

Edgardo always had at least five on the go at any given time. For an article due to be published in the prestigious learned journal *Recherches Sémiotiques*, tentatively entitled 'The Coherence of Incoherence' – a play on the celebrated treatise *Tahafut al-Tahafut* by the twelfth-century Muslim scholar known in the West as Averroes, whose Arab name Ibn Rushd opened up the possibility for the type of puns on the author of *The Satanic Verses* for which Ugo was justly celebrated – he was working at an IBM workstation linked by a fibre optic cable to the University of Bologna's Unix mainframe. Meanwhile, substantial sections of his new metafiction, *Work In Regress*, were rapidly losing shape by being sent via his laptop to a primitive on-line translation site, where they were first mangled into Bulgarian or Welsh and then back again into Italian.

Composition of his contribution to a forthcoming academic seminar on the semiotics of text-messaging at the Université de Paris, on the other hand, took place standing atop a fifteenth century carved stone pulpit removed from the private chapel of a now-demolished palazzo, the text being dictated in a sonorous voice into a Sony digital recorder. Yet another room was kept permanently shuttered, the only light being from a bare hundred-watt bulb dangling above the hardy, ravished desk. It was here, in shirt sleeves and wearing a green eye-shade, that Ugo banged out his weekly column for a glossy, mass-circulation news magazine on a manual upright Olivetti M44 dating from the year of his birth. It was almost impossible to find carbon paper nowadays, so from time to time he had a few dozen boxes flown in from India.

The column generated both money and publicity, but Edgardo already had plenty of both. Indeed, despite his eminent post-modernist credentials, his whole career was living proof that reports of the death of the author had been greatly exaggerated. As for the journalism, he did it for fun, to provide an outlet for his opinions and a way of showing off his versatility. Every writer is all writers, he liked to tell his students, mentioning that Jorge Luis Borges had already pointed out in the 1940s that to attribute the *Imitatio Christi* to Céline or Joyce would serve to renew the work's faded spiritual aspirations, adding that this *esempio* was subversively enriched by the fact that Borges, a slipshod scholar, had probably been thinking of the much more influential *De Imitatione Christi*, and would in any case have attributed both titles to the now discredited Jean de Gerson rather than to Thomas à Kempis. Nevertheless, Borges's idea provided a powerful tool for further deconstructionist analysis. Would not our view of Samuel Beckett's work be both deepened and enriched if it were to be postulated that he had also written a humorous weekly column for the *The Irish Times*, styling himself Myles na Gopaleen and arranging for delivery and payment through an alcoholic Dublin novelist who went under a string of aliases ranging from Brian Ó Nualláin to Flann O'Brien?

They loved him, it went without saying. Ugo's great insight had been that the way to people's hearts was to flatter them. He did it in class, and even more so in the series of erudite fictions which had turned an obscure professor of semiotics at a provincial Italian university into one of the richest and most famous authors in the world. Impress the pants off them with your range of knowledge, then leave them feeling that they're more intelligent and sophisticated than they ever suspected, and they'll always come back for more. With his academic peers worldwide he adopted a subtly different approach, appealing not to their cleverness – they were in no doubt about that – but to their often non-existent charm, humanity and sense of humour. Even they, who didn't much like themselves, let alone anyone else, loved Edgardo.

His phone rang. It was Guerrino Scheda, his lawyer.

'*Ciao Guerrino.* Good news, I hope.'

'I think so. It's a little unusual, and I don't as yet have anything in writing, but I'm reasonably hopeful that I'll be able to pull it off. In which case it would be the perfect solution.'

'Don't be a tease. What's happened?'

'Well, at first I walked into a Berlin Wall of threats and menaces. I wasn't able to speak to Rinaldi personally, but I was given to understand that he's absolutely furious and wants to sue your balls off. He's not interested in a settlement, he claims. Money's not an issue, it's a matter of pride and honour, etcetera. In other words, he wants his day in court and is prepared to pay whatever it costs to have it.'

When the original letter from the legal advisers of Lo Chef's company arrived, threatening an action for 'very substantial' damages on the grounds of personal and professional defamation, Edgardo's initial reaction had been one of disbelief. He had never intended anyone to take his throwaway comment about Rinaldi's cooking skills literally. It was merely an illustration of his basic thesis in the article, namely that we now live not in a consumerist but a post-consumerist society. Our actual needs having been satisfied, we no longer consume products but process. Thus film footage – the photographic record of actual persons, places and times – is increasingly little more than crude raw material to be transformed by computerised post-production techniques.

Ugo had quoted Walter Pater's remark that all art aspires to the condition of music, adding that nowadays all art, including music, aspired to the condition of video games. And in one of those knowing references to the vulgarities of contemporary media culture in which he specialised, he had gone on to point out that no one knew whether Romano Rinaldi, the star of the smash hit TV show *Lo Chef Che Canta e Incanta*, could actually cook at all. Nor did it matter, he had hastened to add, any more than it had mattered when the President of the United States arrived in Iraq on Thanksgiving Day and was photographed in the troop canteen carrying to table what was actually a raw turkey whose skin had been scorched with a blowtorch. Ugo wasn't sure how seriously he really took any of this, but of course the whole point was that in the *cultura post-post-moderna* taking things lightly was of the essence. But apparently Romano Rinaldi saw things differently.

'Suppose you can't pull it off,' he asked the lawyer. 'What are our chances?'

'If it goes to court? Evens, I'd say. Maybe better. After all, you never stated that Rinaldi was a fraud, merely that there's no actual evidence that he can even boil an egg. So we might win.'

'I sense a "but" in the offing.'

'Correct. The two problems with that scenario are that it'll cost a fortune – we're very unlikely to be awarded costs – and generate masses of really stinky publicity whatever the outcome. Rinaldi is certainly a pompous jerk, and for all I know a fraud too, but the fact of the matter is that he's also a national superstar and icon. The people have taken him to their hearts. Particularly women, and you know what they're like when roused. You don't want the latter-day *tricoteuses* on your case. Lo Chef comes across as a cuddly, lovable rogue with a charming light tenor voice who makes the daily grind of cooking seem fun and sexy. You, on the other hand, are an arrogant intellectual who writes pretentious tomes on incomprehensible subjects and secretly despises his fellow men despite a shallow veneer of trendy leftist solidarity.'

'Maybe I should sue you, Scheda.'

'I'm just telling you how it's going to look if we contest this action. We might – *might* – win the judgement, but Rinaldi will win the PR battle and you'll come out of it, at considerable cost, looking like a mean-spirited shit.'

'But you said that he's insisting on going to court. What can I do about it?'

'Show up at the Bologna exhibition centre two days from now.'

'What are you talking about?'

'This is still at the negotiation stage, but I've already roughed it out with his personal assistant, a very intelligent woman called Delia Anselmi. She's totally in agreement and seems to have a lot of influence over Rinaldi. Between the two of us I think we can swing it. But first I need your agreement.'

'To what?'

'Taking part in a cookery contest with Rinaldi during the Enogastexpo food fair that's on there now.'

Edgardo Ugo laughed.

'You must be mad. Or think I am.'

'On the contrary, it's a perfect arrangement for all concerned.'

'But he's bound to win!'

'Of course he is. So you're going to lose a cook-off with the leading celebrity chef in Italy. If you challenged Roger Federer to a game of tennis you'd lose too. How humiliating is that? There are plenty of other aspects of life where you're an acknowledged world champion. All you need to do is show up, shake hands with Lo Chef on stage, maybe join him in a duet – can you sing? – and generally make it clear that the whole affair was just a ridiculous mistake that the media have blown up out of all proportion. In return, he will sign a document that I will prepare, renouncing any legal action whatsoever against you now or in the future. End of story.'

Ugo was silent.

'Plus,' Scheda added, 'and this is the beauty part, the whole show will be broadcast live and as part of the deal I'll arrange for you to have a few minutes solo to camera. There will be multiple repeats later in the day and throughout the weekend. Overall projected viewer numbers are around twenty million.'

'I'll do it.'

Ugo put down the phone. All this talk of food made him realise that he'd forgotten to have lunch. He walked downstairs to the gigantic kitchen and peered despondently into the fridge. There were the remains of the dinner to which he'd invited a group of friends and colleagues the previous weekend, all the dishes being prepared communally from Marinetti's tract on Futurist cooking. As the generous quantity of leftovers indicated, the preparation had been more satisfying than the actual food, but it had all looked very striking and had been beautifully photographed for an article about the event in *La Cucina Italiana* – good publicity for everyone concerned.

He selected a few of the chunks of mortadella and cheese sculpted into letters that had formed part of the dish 'Edible Words', from which all the guests were supposed to eat their own names, then walked through to the former housekeeper's office. This is where he paid his bills, kept his domestic files, and checked his emails. There were very few of the latter today, only twenty-eight new messages. He skimmed through the titles, opening some and deleting others unread. An offer for Lithuanian rights to two of his books, a request from the BBC for him to contribute to a documentary on the cultural significance of professional sport, an invitation to give a series of vapid but very highly-paid lectures in Japan, plus a selection of the usual academic tittle-tattle sent or forwarded by his friends and admirers all over the world.

He clicked open the last unopened email message. The subject header was blank and the 'From' box contained only a Hotmail address consisting of a string of apparently random numbers. As for the message itself, there was no text, just a line drawing – an engraving, rather – of a male hand, the thumb and index finger almost joined to form a circle.

Ugo gazed at it for some time, then walked through to his library, located in the former living and reception rooms of the villa, now knocked through to form one vast and tranquil space. Here he opened a drawer in a handsome rosewood cabinet and consulted the well-thumbed handwritten index cards inside. A minute or so later he had located the position of the volume and, having hauled over the wheeled ladder used for accessing the higher of the eight rows of shelves, was leafing through Andrea de Jorio's classic 1832 text about southern Italian gestures and their origins in classical antiquity.

Yes, there it was: '*Disprezzo*', contempt. Although the tactful Neapolitan cleric had no more than hinted at this, the root significance of the sign was of course blatantly sexual. It was the most powerful non-verbal insult that existed, what de Jorio had termed 'the superlative form' of other offensive gestures.

Basically, someone was telling him to fuck off.

Barefoot and wearing her raincoat as a dressing gown, Flavia was savouring a cigarette and stirring a pan of sauce when there came a pattern of heavy raps at the door. She went to squint at the caller through the fish-eye lens, getting only a general impression of a hat, dark glasses and a heavy overcoat.

'Who is it?'

'Police.'

She took another peek, then unbolted and opened the door. The man flashed a plastic card from his wallet. Flavia made out the word 'Speranza' but nothing more.

'May I come in?' he asked.

He looked more like a secret policeman than the regular sort, thought Flavia, although such men did not present identification or ask permission to come in. But there was only one reason why the police should be interested in her and the other girls living in those rooms, and that was to effect their immediate deportation under the new immigration laws that had been rushed through to satisfy the xenophobic electorate of various politicians whose support was essential to the survival of the governing coalition.

The intruder stood at the centre of the room, looking about him at the mattresses on the floor, the fruit crates used as cupboards, the pot of pasta sauce simmering on the hotplate, the length of blue nylon cord suspended between two bent nails and serving as a communal wardrobe. In an inversion of its normal function, Flavia wrapped the raincoat tightly about her body, still wet and cold from the primitive shower in the opposite corner.

'Nice place,' the man remarked.

This was too obvious a provocation to merit a reply.

'You sharing?'

Flavia shook her head. There was just a chance of saving the other girls, if she could somehow get word to them before they came home. Didn't they have to allow you a phone call here in Europe? The man was staring at their meagre possessions, in full view all around. There was still a chance, though, since these added up to less than a quarter of what the average Italian woman would have regarded as the basic minimum.

The policeman took a studio photograph from the inside pocket of his double-breasted coat and showed it to Flavia.

'You know this person,' he said.

She recognised Rodolfo's flatmate immediately, although she had never seen him wearing a jacket and tie, but shook her head again. The intruder replaced the photograph and produced a shiny metal hip flask from which he took a long gurgling drink.

'Sure you do,' he said, wiping his lips. 'Name's Vincenzo. Vincenzo Amadori.'

He swapped the flask for a packet of cigarettes from yet another pocket of his capacious coat.

'Mind if I smoke?'

She shook her head again.

'Want one?'

Her instinct was to refuse – tell nothing, take nothing – but a much older superstition reminded her that three denials brought bad luck. The packet was labelled Camels and the cigarette the man lit for her had a pleasant toasty flavour. American imports, she thought inconsequentially. Definitely the secret police. She decided to call him Dragos.

'Sure you know him,' the intruder insisted. 'Number seventy-four Via Marsala, second floor at the back.'

Flavia realised that further evasion was in vain. Clearly she had been followed.

'I am see him there I think,' she declared in a laborious chant.

'Hey, it talks as well!' Dragos remarked with a jocular leer. 'Tell me you mix a mean martini, darling, and you've got yourself a date. Actually, all you need to do is sit down and cross your legs.'

He looked around hopefully, but chairs were among the many items of furniture the room lacked.

'You go there to see him?' Dragos continued. 'Or is it the other kid?'

'The other.'

A sharp nod.

'Smart girl. Strictly between you, me and anyone who may be listening in behind these cardboard walls, our little Prince Vince is bad news.'

'I already know these. But he is not a prince I think.'

The secret policeman's attention had seemingly wandered again, this time to the electric hotplate that was the household's only cooking facility. He walked over and sniffed the simmering sauce appreciatively.

'Have you ever met any of his friends?' he remarked in a tone of studied indifference.

'Of this Vincenzo?'

'The very same.'

Drago sucked at his cigarette.

'He's fallen into bad company, you see. His parents are very worried.'

'My friend he is not bad company.'

'Mattioli? No, he's okay, for a student. But there's this crew that Amadori hangs out with at football matches. They're a different story.'

'These I never see.'

'Never, eh?'

Dragos picked up a spoon, dipped it into the pasta sauce and slurped down the contents, turning to Flavia with a patronising smirk that was abruptly wiped from his face. He dropped the spoon and clutched his throat, then doubled over and began bawling incoherently.

Flavia ran to the washbasin and filled the toothglass with water, but the sufferer had already grabbed a beaker of colourless fluid from a nearby shelf and downed it in one. The result was a series of piercing shrieks which blasted openings into that wing of the palace which the Princess had ordered to be abandoned and sealed up years before.

'Merda di merda di merda di merda di merda di merda di . . .'

It was only after administering a lengthy course of plain yoghurt diluted with lemon juice that Flavia was able to get her visitor into a fit state to leave, which by then was all he showed any desire to do. Unfortunately the interruption left her no time to complete and then eat the late lunch she had been eagerly anticipating before going to work. She was particularly resentful about this since the sauce – despite the unprintable things the secret policeman had said about it – was a personal favourite which she could only prepare on very rare occasions when the necessary ingredient was to hand.

There were few enough things that Flavia missed about her native country, but the relish which formed the basis of this sauce was one. It consisted of sliced red and yellow goatshorn peppers, robustly hot and subtly sweet, steeped in oil with garlic and lemon zest and mysterious spices. The wonderfully intense flavour suffused your entire system for hours afterwards, warming and reinvigorating both flesh and spirit. It was a perfect pick-me-up for this vicious cold spell that had lasted for weeks, and Flavia had been overjoyed when six large and priceless jars emerged from the parcel she had received the day before from the woman who had been her closest friend during their long childhood years in the House of Joy.

But enough water to cook the pasta would take at least twenty minutes to come to the boil on the feeble electric ring, and in half an hour she was due at work. The managerial underling she had to deal with was an obnoxious little tyrant who had already made it abundantly clear that he regarded women like Flavia as expendable casual labour, and that the least infringement of her verbal terms of engagement would result in instant dismissal. So she mopped up as much of the delicious sauce as she could by dunking chunks of day-old bread into it, happily chomping it down. Why on earth the policeman had made such a fuss about the mouthful he'd tasted was utterly beyond her, although the remains of a glass of the homemade plum brandy that Viorica had also sent was probably not the ideal antidote.

Nevertheless, she felt that she had scored a point in some way. By the time he finally left, Dragos had been very tractable, indeed almost tearfully grateful for Flavia's ministrations, and had insisted on leaving her his phone number with a line about her 'being well rewarded' for any information she passed on about Vincenzo Amadori. Flavia would of course never have dreamt of voluntarily telling the police anything about anyone, let alone a person associated, however insignificantly, with Rodolfo, but she definitely felt that she had won that particular encounter, and arrived at the bus stop in the freezing gloom with a light, lively smile on her lips.

The subject of Romano Rinaldi's private life had generated a good deal of speculation, the more so in that next to nothing was known about it. For that matter, he himself barely knew anything definite about his true origins and – as he had explained to his publicist when Lo Chef's growing fame made it necessary to hire one – what he did know, or suspected, was far too lurid to form a basis for the type of public persona he wished to create.

The publicist had listened to a rambling account of an informal and peripatetic childhood under the tutelage of a number of 'aunts', all of whom had originally formed part of the female entourage of a certain Italian pop idol of the 1960s whose star had now faded, but who was still alive and known to be extremely litigious. One by one these guardians had disappeared from the scene, until the last had brought the pubescent Romano with her when she joined a religious cult based in an abandoned complex of troglodytic dwellings out in the wilds somewhere east of Potenza.

At this point the publicist – a smugly jovial man with the air of a retired circus ringmaster – held up his hand.

'Has anyone from that period ever tried to contact you?' he asked.

'No.'

'Any family members still living?'

'None that I know of.'

'If someone shows up claiming to be related to you, do we have deniability?'

'Why not? I can't even prove anything myself.'

The publicist beamed and released a long, lingering sigh.

'I've been waiting all my life for someone like you,' he said.

An alternative version of the star's early years had duly been invented, featuring a poor but happy upbringing in working-class Rome, with a classic salt-of-the-earth mother who ruled her numerous brood with a rod of iron but saw them through the hard times, of which needless to say there were many, and above all served up the delicious, nourishing traditional meals that had first awakened the young Romano's interest in cooking. For a time, an out-of-work actress had been hired to represent this redoubtable personage, but she had threatened to sell her story to a celebrity gossip mag and had had to be bought off and written out of the plot. After that the surrogate family had been kept strictly off-stage, ostensibly to protect the sanctity of Lo Chef's private life, which was particularly precious to him following his mother's tragic stroke.

Romano's actual roots had however left their mark on him, not least in his conviction that the only thing worth achieving was the long-term certainty of short-term pleasure, and that any attempt to analyse or understand life was a complete waste of time. He was therefore unaware of the irony involved in the fact that once the money started rolling in to the point where he could invest in the construction of new apartment blocks, he himself had chosen to live exactly where he had grown up: illegally in a hole in the ground. The owners of properties such as his typically had a phantom *abusivo* dwelling constructed on the roof and classified for rating purposes as a storage facility; Romano had done something similar, but deep underground, and it was in this bunker that he was now planning the opening blitzkreig of his total war against Professor Edgardo Ugo.

To be honest, he was still furious with Delia, although a smidgin or two of the good stuff had phased his anger down

from the screaming fit he had treated her to when she originally pitched the idea to him after the recording session that
morning. But his core position hadn't changed one iota, and
the sooner she realised this the better. He had no interest in a
negotiated solution to Ugo's scandalous provocation. What he
wanted was the arsehole's arse on a plate, and Delia's job, as
his highly-paid gofer, was to jiggle her brisket cutely under his
nose and enquire sweetly if he wanted fries with that, not tell
him that he should have ordered something else.

The computer emitted a soft gong-like sound, indicating the
arrival of an email. Sensing his mood starting to darken again,
Rinaldi quickly snorted another line. Cooking might be problematic for him, but when it came to coking he was a wizard.
He crossed the minimalistically furnished expanses of the concrete coffer-dam that had been constructed amid the founda-
tions of the apartment block and glared at the screen.

I can't take your refusal as absolute, Romano, there's just too much
at stake. This was potentially a great crisis. I've turned it into an
equally great opportunity. I completely understand your justifiable
feelings of hurt, but the fact remains that you'd be a fool not to grab
this chance of both clearing your name and garnering positive publicity for the show, the products and the Lo Chef brand name.
FWIW, the whole team is in agreement on this.

Rinaldi sat down at the keyboard and fired off his reply.

I don't do live.

The little bitch was obviously handling this in real time – her
own job was on the line, of course, although so far she hadn't
mentioned this – because she came right back at him.

The jury will be rigged. I explained all this to you when we met. I've
already got five judges signed up and am working on the rest. You

will also be informed of the list of ingredients in advance – in fact we can more or less dictate them – and will be intensively coached by Righi as usual. By the time the show goes on stage even you will be able to whip up an acceptable pasta dish within the time limit. You have everything to gain and nothing to lose. For God's sake think about it.

He let the coke reply to this one.

There's nothing to think about. Where I grew up, down in the streets, among people who had nothing but their pride, we had a saying. 'If you lose your money, nothing is lost. If you lose your health, much is lost. If you lose your honour, all is lost.' This arrogant bastard has impugned my honour. He shall pay for that.

Romano clicked this off and then fiddled around until he had programmed the stress-reducing 'Pure White Noise' audio file. Barely had the unvarying swishing pervaded the room than the computer gonged again. Rinaldi was tempted to ignore it, but he knew that this issue had to be resolved, and far better by email than in person.

Fine, go right ahead. FYI, our legal consultant has advised us that our chances of winning a court case are at best fifty-fifty. Technically speaking, Ugo did not libel you. His comments were simply a 'hypothetical illustrative example' designed to sex up one of his the-way-we-live-now pieces. But if you sue, he will hire the very best lawyers in the country and quite possibly a few muck-raking hacks to dig around and see what they can come up with. Disgruntled former employees, etc. Remember little Placida, who turned out not to be? It could get really nasty. At best we'll win a 'moral victory' that no one will care about, which will cost a fortune in fees and still leave everyone wondering whether you can actually cook or not. But once you have demonstrated your skills and superiority live on TV at the Bologna food fair – and don't forget that the contest is sewn up in your favour whatever happens in the kitchen – then the prospects for your future career are assured, not just here in Italy but world-wide. Professor Ugo may be an arrogant bastard, but he is also a huge international personality. Out-takes from this event are going to be shown on hundreds of foreign channels, maybe thousands. You know those little feel-good stories they stick in at the end of the news after the politics and wars and atrocities? 'And now, on a lighter note . . .' You're going to own that slot, Romano. I personally guarantee you that if you accept the opportunity that I've set up then by the end of the year *Lo Chef Che Canta e Incanta* will be global, and all the spin-off branded products along with it. We're talking potentially millions. And one more thing, for what it may be worth. If you pigheadedly insist on going to court despite all the above, consider me fired.

Feeling his resolution beginning to weaken, Rinaldi sidled over to the modest kitchenette, where he occasionally warmed up a cup of instant soup or burnt a defrosted slice of bread under the grill, and snapped open a bottle of Coke. He well remembered the days before his current success, when he had eked out an exiguous livelihood voicing jingles for advertisements to be aired on local radio stations. It had been a studio director for one of these who had come up with the original idea for the Lo Chef show, and originally it had been intended as little more than a joke. But the director had contacts at various television production companies, and after a few embellishments, such as the singing, had been added to the pitch, one of these had agreed to make a pilot at a discounted fee refundable if they could find a broadcaster willing to take it on.

They had, and the ratings had been good enough for the TV station to come back for a mini-series of six episodes. Ratings had climbed by leaps and bounds with each screening – all word of mouth – and Rinaldi got a contract to do a full series for the rest of the year. When that expired, he was in a position to negotiate a very much more lucrative contract with the nation's most-watched channel, plus a prime-time slot right after the smash hit *Filthy Rich Stupid Sluts* reality show. At first the friend involved had run the production company, but the momentum of the product had soon exhausted his meagre skills and Romano Rinaldi had reluctantly been forced to dispense with his services.

Like all ideas of genius, this one was basically very simple. Italian cooking was dying. Not at the restaurant level, but in the home. Men had never dreamt of learning how to cook, and nowadays most women were too tired and preoccupied to do so. In any case, they wouldn't know how. The oral tradition that had passed down recipes and techniques from mother to daughter for countless centuries had virtually died out, along with the extended family and stay-at-home wives.

Hence Lo Chef's appeal. His warm, unthreatening, campily flirty screen persona tapped deeply into his viewership's culinarily challenged subconscious, allaying its anxieties and sense of inadequacy while validating its dream and aspirations. The popularity of his show was not based on educating the younger generation in the basics of putting food on the table, although the scriptwriters were constantly reminded that their target audience included people who thought that milk came fresh from the cow at 5°C, and even those who had never realised that cows were involved at all. But Lo Chef's viewers didn't want instruction, they wanted glamour, a few 'authentic' tips from the top, and above all a bit of fun.

This was where the singing came in. Sections of the recipe, directions, ingredients, preparation methods all floated out in Rinaldi's very serviceable light tenor – another link to his childhood, and possibly even his parentage – to the melodies of famous operas and popular songs. Everyone relaxed and smiled as the chubby, lovable TV personality whipped up another stunning, authentic dish 'from our incomparable and timeless gastronomic tradition', accompanied by two scantily clad, inanely grinning bimbettes with pneumatic boobs who got the male audience on board while giving the average housewife the satisfaction of jeering at their utter incompetence, for which they were always being indulgently scolded by the star, his eyes raised to heaven.

It had been a dynamite concept, and one he had managed carefully. By now he was less interested in direct revenue from the TV station than in exposure for the ever-expanding line of products marketed under the *Lo Chef Che Canta e Incanta* trademark. This was the sweetest aspect of the whole enterprise, since it required no effort on Rinaldi's part whatsoever. Even initially, all he had had to do was to find a reasonably good product available at a knockdown wholesale price, then contact the producer and make a bid for exclusive retail rights. Now, of course, the producers contacted him. He was deluged with offers. Then it was just a matter of hiring some marketing hack to write a lyrical blurb to print on the label beneath a cheery image of the star in his white coat and chef's hat, his hand held out and mouth open as he reached for a high C, and ship it out to the supermarkets.

He had started with the Coop chain that controlled most mass food outlets in central Italy, then moved on to Conad and the other national chains. He knew just how women felt as they trudged up and down the aisles in those smelly, crowded food marts. They longed for the personal contact and preferential treatment they got at the small, old-fashioned shops, but doing the rounds of all those was just too much of a bother after a hard day at work. The supermarkets were quick, convenient and cheap, but they felt chilly and impersonal. So when Signora Tizia spotted Romano's cheerful, friendly features on the distinctive red and yellow label, she reached for it as if he had been holding her arm. No need for expensive hit-or-miss advertising either. The shelves of the studio where he recorded his show were stacked with those very same products, all with the labels turned outwards and sporting the Lo Chef logo that was also back-projected on the false rear wall of the set. And whenever a new product was introduced to the range, Rinaldi would extol its virtues in an extended aria based on the rhapsodic publicity gush.

He took another swig of Coke, then headed back to the glass-topped table. He knew he was overdoing it, but he had a tough decision to make. Quite some time passed before he realised that he had in fact made it, and he reached for the phone.

'All right, I'll do it.'

There was an audible intake of breath at the other end.

'That's wonderful, Romano! You've absolutely made the correct decision. But time is pressing. You need to come to Bologna this evening, okay? As in right now. I'll arrange a car and book a hotel and email you the details ASAP. And once again, congratulations!'

As a parting shot on learning of Zen's imminent departure from Lucca, Gemma had reminded him of their collusion in the death of Roberto Lessi and the subsequent disposal of his body at sea. In his view, this had been a clumsy manoeuvre – Gemma was brandishing a weapon they both knew was far too dangerously destructive to be used. She would have done better to have reminded him that on the occasion to which she had referred, when the truth about his identity had finally emerged, he had promised her that whatever happened he would never tell her any more lies.

Despite itself being a barefaced whopper of some considerable magnitude, this had passed without comment, perhaps because at the time Zen had believed it himself. And until recently the atmosphere of the relationship, seemingly charged with infinite promise, had indeed appeared to make lies an irrelevant anachronism. Incredibly enough, he really had believed that in getting together with Gemma, and in the move from his apartment in Rome to hers in Lucca that resulted, he had magically reinvented himself. The events of recent months, however, had returned a different verdict, namely that this belief had been just another coil in the spiral of illusions that his life had come to resemble.

As with the gradual deterioration of the body, it was hard to say exactly when it had all started, but the rows were coming more frequently, and with them the lies. A trivial example had occurred when Gemma had asked why Zen was going to Bologna, mistakenly believing this to be a free choice on his part. 'Years ago I was stationed in the city and I loved it,' he'd replied. It was true that he couldn't wait to leave, but it was not going back to Bologna that he was looking forward to; any-where would have done. During the journey up in the train, he tried to remember the last time he had been posted to the city, some time during the 1970s, the terrorist *anni di piombo*, when 'red' Bologna had been one of the hotbeds of unrest. But that side of police work was handled by the DIGOS and other specialised anti-terrorist units, while Zen, as a very junior officer attached to the criminal investigation department, had been left to deal with the usual routine crimes committed by people whose interest was not in overthrowing the state but in lining their pockets or settling some personal dispute.

All he could recall were isolated incidents, such as the time he'd followed a small-time gangster to a tough suburban bar, where his target was menaced by a rival. Zen's man responded by pulling out a flick-knife and driving it, almost up to the hilt, into his own leg. Then, without the slightest flicker of expression, he turned to the other thug and said, 'That's what I'm capable of doing to myself, Giorgio. Imagine what I would be capable of doing to you.' The aggressor looked like he was about to faint and left in extreme haste, after which the gang-ster pulled out the knife, replaced it in his pocket, then rolled up his trouser leg and removed his prosthetic limb, to the gen-eral merriment of the company.

Or the time he went to interview a woman who claimed that her ex-husband had been stalking her. She'd sounded rather highly strung on the phone, and when Zen got to her apart-ment and asked some rather detailed and intimate questions she had first slapped his face, knuckles out, then burst into a lengthy and deafening fit of tears, and finally begged him to come to bed with her. In the end he'd agreed, and the results were so satisfactory that the following morning he'd suggest-ed that they repeat the experience. To which the lady had icily replied, 'You were Tuesday. This is Wednesday.'

And then there was the occasion when he had chased a notorious drug dealer and suspected murderer down the twisty, arcaded streets of the city centre, only to have the man disappear in front of his eyes. When Zen finally located the open door through which he must have turned, he was met by an expanse of black liquid a couple of metres below, one of the 'lost' canals of Bologna, now buried beneath buildings and car parks. Ripples on the surface of the water showed the escape route that the fugitive had chosen, but even at that relatively young age Zen had felt no inclination to follow.

But these were mere anecdotes, and the incidents involved might have happened elsewhere. What was lacking was any overall sense of the city as an entity in its own right, unique and unconfoundable with any other. The thing that struck him most today, in the brief taxi ride from the station to the centre, was the glaring comparison with Florence, so near and yet a world away. Bologna was already the north, home of hard workers, hearty eaters, heavy drinkers and dank, dour, depressing winters lacking any of the mitigating hints of vernal promise that regions south of the Apennines always kept up their sleeves. Unlike Zen's other postings, moreover, the strongest impression this city seemed to have left was the efficiency of its civic mechanisms, which scored the highest possible mark on his rule-of-thumb criterion for such things, viz. the public garbage skips in the street are emptied (a) every day, (b) every week, (c) once in a while, (d) never. That and the food, which Zen sat down to sample as soon as he had installed himself at the hotel recommended by his cab driver as being conveniently close to the Questura. He had also recommended a restaurant, where Zen ate his way through an appetiser of superb *culatello*, that almost unobtainable delicacy which a fellow officer had once described as 'Parma ham for grown-ups', followed by deliciously thin and eggy layers of lasagna with the famous Bolognese *ragù*, and finally rabbit cooked in white wine and balsamic vinegar, a rich feast made palatable by a pleasantly astringent red wine still lively from its recent fermentation.

Considered merely from a nutritional point of view, this one meal represented more calories than his average daily intake, although he still had a hard time persuading the waiter that a dish of creamy baked custard would not provide a suitable conclusion. Instead he had a double *caffè ristretto* at a nearby bar and then set off to face whatever welcome awaited him at the Questura. This building was an example of Fascist grandiloquence and triumphalism at its most menacingly turgid, a massive temple to the power of the state out of all proportion to the modest piazzetta in which it was situated. Perhaps Bologna had been a left-wing hotbed even then. Certainly the message being sent couldn't have been clearer: behind the boys in blue were the men in black.

The interior was on a scarcely less awesome scale, but Zen's reception turned out to be reassuringly low-key. His contact was an officer named Salvatore Brunetti, whose manner resembled that of the many doctors he had encountered during his stay in the Rome clinic, who always gave the impression that Zen was a malingering crank who had nothing the matter wrong with him but must be humoured to prevent the possibility of violent outbursts.

'So what exactly is your mission here?' the Bologna police officer asked once the usual courtesies had been observed.

'Perhaps it would be best if I tell you what it isn't,' Zen replied. 'For example, I'm not here to intervene, take control, undermine your authority, nor above all to snitch on you to my superiors in Rome.'

Salvatore Brunetti looked back at him with the same polite, distant, mildly amused air.

'My remit is very specific,' Zen continued firmly, 'and I intend to honour it to the letter. Given the identity of the victim and the circumstances under which he died, this is clearly going to be an extremely high-profile case, and has already generated a lot of media exposure and comment. My superiors at the Viminale naturally want to be kept informed of developments as they happen, in real time, with a view to exploiting them to maximum political effect if they are positive and minimising negative fallout as soon as possible if not. They have instructed me to facilitate that process. And that's all.'

Brunetti waited a moment, then vaguely smiled.

'That's very frank of you, *vice-questore*.'

'Too frank, you mean. Suspiciously so, in fact. But it happens to be true. I am of a slightly older generation than you, Dottor Brunetti, and I occasionally allow myself the luxury of saying what I actually mean. I am doing so now. I can quite understand that you don't necessarily believe me, but frankly it would save us both a lot of time and bother if you did.'

Caught off guard, his interlocutor laughed nervously.

'But of course I believe you!'

With a fastidious finger he indicated the thick file of documents on the teak desk between them.

'Well, you'll find everything that we know at this point in there. And if I can help to clarify or amplify any points involved, please don't hesitate to ask.'

Zen picked up the file and put it away in his briefcase.

'Thank you,' he said. 'I'll give it my fullest attention as soon as possible. In the meantime, could you perhaps give me a brief summary of the basic facts?'

Brunetti nodded vigorously.

'It's quite straightforward. The autopsy and forensic examinations have confirmed that Lorenzo Curti was murdered in the driver's seat of his car about an hour before the discovery of the vehicle by one of our patrols. He was first shot through the heart with a 7.62 millimetre bullet, which was recovered, then stabbed in the chest with a Parmesan cutting knife which was left in situ and also recovered. The presence of the latter item suggests foreknowledge of the victim's family and business origins.'

'And premeditation.'

'Indeed. Curti had attended the away match between his football team and Ancona. After the game he spent some time with the manager and players in the dressing room, then left alone to drive home. The electronic toll records show that his Audi saloon entered the autostrada system at Ancona Nord shortly before seven that evening and exited at Bologna San Lázzaro just over ninety minutes later, very shortly before he was killed.'

'Would that have been his normal route?'

'No. He lived outside Parma. His reason for leaving the motorway there is still unclear. It's a moderately rough area at that time of night, but the element of premeditation and the implicit message sent by the post-mortem stabbing with the cheese cutter virtually rules out the possibility that this was an opportunistic or casual crime committed by some hitchhiker, drug dealer or pimp. In fact it's virtually certain that the killer was known to Curti, and extremely probable that they had either made an appointment to meet at the scene of the murder or had travelled back together from Ancona. Why else, on a dark, cold evening, should Curti have left the autostrada at San Lázzaro instead of continuing straight on to join the A1 for Parma?'

'So you've been looking for someone among the victim's social or business contacts with a motive to kill him?' suggested Zen helpfully.

'That's naturally what we have been doing,' Brunetti replied. 'But so far without result.'

'On the contrary! It turns out that just about everyone Curti knew personally or professionally had a reason to wish him dead. As you probably know, his business empire has virtually crumbled overnight, the shares are now worth next to nothing, and our friends over at the Guardia di Finanza are starting a serious fraud investigation which will almost certainly result in jail sentences for many of those involved – including Curti himself – had this not happened.'

'But now he won't be able to testify.'

'Tempting hypothesis, isn't it?'

There was a silence.

'Unfortunately . . .'

Brunetti let the word hang heavily for a moment.

'The bad news is that virtually all the potential suspects were either at the game, out with friends, or at home in the bosom of their families. Of the rest, several were abroad and one was in labour.'

'A woman?' Zen queried.

Brunetti kindly ignored him.

'Meanwhile the Curti clan have issued a statement hotly denying any insider involvement, and offering a one million euro reward for the arrest and conviction of the killer. In short, we have a vast list of potential suspects, but no hard evidence against any of them, while almost all seem to have unbreakable alibis.'

'What about the forensic tests on the car? Fibres, hairs and so on.'

'Masses of it, ninety-nine per cent canine. Curti kept a Labrador. And swathes of fingerprints, too, but even if we made a match it would prove nothing. Almost all the suspects will have been in that Audi at one time or another, most of them very recently.'

'And the gun?'

'A spent cartridge case was found in the car, suggesting an autoloading pistol. It's a rimless, brass-coated steel model with as yet unidentified headstamps, probably of foreign origin. Ballistics ran the markings on the bullet through the system. Nothing. It looks like a virgin.'

'A hired assassin? It sounds as though plenty of people wanted Curti dead, just as long as they had an unbreakable alibi. And there's any number of under-employed people with the necessary skills and equipment in eastern Europe these days.'

'It's conceivable,' Brunetti acknowledged.

Zen stood up, clasping his briefcase.

'Well, sounds like an interesting challenge. Please let me know if anything new should emerge. At any hour of the day or night. Otherwise I'll just try to keep out of your way.'

He was walking with bowed head along the interminable corridors of the Questura when he heard running footsteps behind him. A young man in patrolman's uniform appeared.

'Dottor Zen! Forgive me, but we just passed and I recognised you.'

Zen stared at him blankly. The patrolman touched his cap.

'Bruno Nanni, *dottore*. I was your driver during your visit last year to the Alto Adige.'

Zen smiled broadly.

'So it all worked out?' he said with genuine pleasure.

'My transfer came through about ten days later. Incredible, eh? And all thanks to you, *capo!*'

Zen made a self-deprecatory gesture.

'I had a word with a certain person, but that sort of thing doesn't always work.'

'Well, it worked this time, *dottore*, and I can't thank you enough. But what are you doing here in Bologna, if you don't mind my asking?'

'Just another routine job. A temporary secondment to

review and assess an ongoing case.'

'Have you any plans for this evening?'

'Not a thing.'

'Then you might care to go to the stadium.'

'The football stadium?'

Nanni nodded.

'The club's holding a memorial service for Lorenzo Curti. Funnily enough, I was the one who discovered the body. Anyway, all the players will be there, the rest of the staff, and of course the supporters. They'll all pay tribute, in their different ways, to the late president of Bologna FC.'

'Doesn't really sound like my sort of thing, Bruno.'

'It might be interesting from a professional point of view,' Nanni remarked, rather too casually.

'In what way?'

'This case that you've come to look into. It has to be the Curti murder, right? The Ministry isn't going to send a senior man like yourself up here for anything else that's happened lately. Well, the event itself may be pretty dreary, but the stadium will be packed with every diehard fan in the city.'

'So?'

Bruno Nanni smiled mysteriously.

'What I've heard from friends is that a certain individual, one of the craziest and most violent of the *ultra* mob, has been putting the word about that he killed Curti. He'll certainly be there tonight, and I know the bar where that gang goes to booze it up afterwards. It might just be worth your while taking a look at him.'

Zen weighed up the options. After all, what did he have to lose? The only alternative was to eat a solitary dinner and then spend a lonely evening in his hotel room watching television. He might even get desperate enough to read the copy of the file that Brunetti had given him.

'Very well. I'm staying at the Hotel Roma, just round the corner.'

'I'll pick you up just before six, *dottore.*'

A blinding flash.

'Smile, you're on Candid Camera!'

Vincenzo straddled the doorway in an extravagantly debonair pose, one leg cocked up behind him and a tiny metallic object held to his eye. Another flash of halogen brilliance. Vincenzo laughed and tossed the object across the room to Rodolfo, who put down his book and just managed to make the catch.

'Wicked, huh?'

Rodolfo turned the thing over. It seemed to be some sort of camera, but smaller than any he had seen, or indeed imagined possible. But Vincenzo was clearly high, so he decided to appear underwhelmed.

'Very clever,' he remarked coolly. 'How much did it cost?'

Vincenzo laughed uproariously for some time.

'Oh, I picked it up last night after the game. Along with another little toy that's not bad either. What can I tell you? I got lucky. I finally got lucky.'

He started pacing restlessly about the room, occasionally kicking the furniture.

'Have you been snorting Ritalin again?' asked Rodolfo.

'None of your fucking business. You're not my mother.'

Rodolfo closed the book he had been leafing through and gently palpated the sturdy, plain, well-worn leather binding. He must return it today, he thought. Volumes as rare and precious as this were not supposed to be removed from the university library, but graduate students of Professor Edgardo Ugo enjoyed certain privileges.

'I'm trying to study, Vincenzo,' he lied.

His flatmate grinned aggressively.

'So are you planning to just sit here all evening reading a musty old book and then scribble some shit for that cocksucking prof to sneer at? Jesus, what a pathetic life!'

'At least I'm getting laid.'

'Yeah, by some illegal immigrant from Christ knows where with a temporary job as a cleaner. Congratulations, *terrone*! You'll make a great couple.'

Rodolfo was on his feet in a second. He grabbed Vincenzo by the shoulder and slammed him against the wall.

'Take that back!'

Vincenzo looked stunned.

'Fuck! Can't you take a joke?'

Rodolfo held him pinned against the wall, staring the other intensely in the eyes until he looked away.

'Fucking southerners,' complained Vincenzo. 'Bunch of freaking crazies.'

'Quite right, my friend. And if you ever allow yourself one more insulting remark about my girlfriend, or for that matter my people, you'll find out exactly how crazy we can be.'

Vincenzo shook his head weakly.

'*Va bene, va bene. Basta, oh!*'

Rodolfo nodded sharply and with significance, then released the other man. Vincenzo shook himself with a certain hauteur.

'Anyway, you're not the only ones who can be a little crazy. It's just that up here in the north we don't make empty threats.'

Rodolfo went back to the sofa and opened Andrea de Jorio's *La mimica degli antichi investigata nel gestire napoletano* at the illustration he had been examining earlier, marvelling at the quality and detail of the engraving.

'Meaning what?' he muttered through a long yawn.

'Meaning this evening's service of tribute down at the stadium.'

'You speak in riddles.'

Vincenzo laughed scornfully.

'If you ever got your head out of the library and into the real world, you'd know the answer.'

'Unfortunately I'm not a spoilt brat like you, Vincenzo. I can't afford to play at being the eternal student. My father has spent a lot of money sending me up here to get a degree. He naturally expects to see some return on that investment.'

And is going to be shattered and furious when he finds out that I have pissed it away, he thought.

'All that interpretation shit you study with Ugo?' Vincenzo retorted. 'Well, interpret this! Someone killed Lorenzo Curti because he bought our team, with all its glorious history, for a song, then let all the best players go and was too cheap to get replacements. He's been screwing us over for years, and last night he paid the price.'

'They said on TV it was probably to do with his business dealings.'

Vincenzo shrugged impatiently.

'What do those jerks know? Anyway, the important thing is the bastard's dead, and there isn't a true-hearted Bologna fan who isn't totally over the moon. So of course we're all going along to this memorial thing they're putting on, only – get this! – we're going to laugh all the way through it. Sure, I'm a little stoned. The others will be too. We won't do anything outrageous, but up there in the stands we'll be holding our own private commemorative service. And I promise you, the tone will be rather different from the official one down on the pitch. So give me that jacket of mine you stole.'

Rodolfo retrieved the battered, black leather garment and handed it to Vincenzo, who stomped out of the apartment without another word, slamming the front door behind him.

Blissfully solitary once more, Rodolfo took one last lingering look at the *Disprezzo* engraving that he had scanned and downloaded – using the university's state-of-the-art technical facilities – and then forwarded to Professor Ugo. Knowledge of his email address and mobile phone number was another of the privileges that Ugo made available to graduate students.

Not that Rodolfo was one any more. His tutor had made it very clear that he had been barred from attending the seminar course and stood no chance of receiving his final degree, although like any other member of the public he was at perfect liberty to attend the professor's celebrated weekly lectures, the next of which was tomorrow. Rodolfo smiled reflectively. Maybe he would go along and hold his own 'private commemorative service', just like Vincenzo and the rest of the yobs at the stadium tonight. Nothing outrageous, as Vincenzo had put it, but he might put in an appearance. He'd have to go back to the uni soon anyway, if only to return the Andrea de Jorio book and all the others that he had borrowed over the past months, most of which were long overdue.

He walked through to his bedroom and was scanning the shelves for the necessary titles when the phone rang.

'It's your old dad, Rodolfo. Just my usual weekly call. Like to keep in touch, you know.'

'Yes, of course.'

'So how are things?'

'Fine, dad. Fine.'

'Wish I could say the same.'

'What's happened?'

'Oh, nothing really.'

The voice paused.

'At least, nothing I want to talk about over the phone. You understand?'

'What's happened?'

The resulting silence was finally broken by a bitter guffaw.

'What do they teach you up there at the university?' his father mused quietly, as though to himself. 'You know nothing. Less than you did when you were ten. Five, even. Nothing, nothing . . .'

The voice died away.

'I know a few things,' Rodolfo replied truculently, hoping that he wouldn't be asked to provide an example.

But now his father sounded contrite.

'Of course you do, of course. You're very learned, I'm sure. You must forgive me, it's just . . .'

'What, dad?'

'Nothing. Just keep talking, that calms me. It's probably just that I've been overworking.'

'On what?'

'Oh, it doesn't matter.'

'Tell me!'

'Well, we've been rebuilding a retaining wall on a bend in the road up past Monte Iacovizzo, up there in the Gargano. It's in the national park, so we have to use the original granite blocks. An absolute bitch. We've been there all month, and we're not done yet. It's going to be way over budget, but it's for the government so of course there's no problem about cost overruns.'

Silence fell.

'What's a retaining wall?' asked Rodolfo artlessly.

His father laughed harshly.

'Don't pretend you give a damn!'

'I do.'

Another long silence.

'Well,' his father began hesitantly, as though still suspicious of a trap, 'basically they support unstable ground. And they're always problematic, especially old ones like the one we're mending.'

'Why?'

'Because they defy the laws of gravity and of soil mechanics. There are so many ways they can fail.'

'Such as what?'

'Sliding, foundation failure, you name it. Overturning is the most common. What most people don't realise is that mortar isn't a glue, it's just to level out the irregularities in the stone blocks and keep the pressure diagram constant. That sort of wall is a simple gravity structure, so you need to calculate the overturning moment.'

'You can predict when it will fall down?'

His father laughed again, with indulgent contempt this time.

'Not that kind of moment, idiot! The outward push at a given distance from the base. The weight of the blocks times the horizontal distance from the front of the wall gives the restoring moment. That obviously has to be greater than the overturning moment if the thing's going to stand up.'

'I never knew anything about this,' Rodolfo remarked.

His father laughed cannily.

'You're taking the piss, aren't you? Patronising your dumb old dad banging on about stuff the Romans knew as if it was breaking news!'

'It's news to me.'

'I'm sure it is, but why should you care?'

'What about failure?' his son replied.

'It can happen for lots of reasons. Rising water levels during the rainy season, seasonal shrinkage and swelling.'

Rodolfo murmured his comprehension.

'So failure is the key to everything,' he said.

'How do you mean?'

'Well, the possibility of failure. That's the truth maker, as philosophers say. The only authentic tasks are those at which you can fail.'

A silence fell. No, there was a sound of the sea, or maybe the soughing of a breeze in the oak grove around the house. Then he thought that his father was laughing quietly. But as the sound went on, Rodolfo realised that he was weeping.

'What's the matter, dad?' he cried with genuine alarm.

'I'm just lonely. Since your mother died, I've been all alone, and with so many problems, professional and personal. I want you here, but all I get is a disembodied voice down the phone line. I hate telephones, I hate computers, I hate this technology that is stealing our souls! Laugh at me all you like, the fact remains that I want you to be here. Here in Puglia, here at home. You, my only son.'

Yet another silence.

'Now do you understand?' his father asked.

'Well, I'm not sure. I mean, what exactly do you have in mind?'

'No, you don't,' his father retorted, plainly ashamed of having let his feelings show for the first time. 'Your problem, Rodolfo, is that you've been educated beyond your intelligence. What the hell is this *semiotica* all about, anyway? Can you explain it to me the way I just explained retaining walls to you? If you have to waste more of your time and my money at university, why not go the whole hog and study *ottica*? That way you could at least make some money as an eye doctor when you finally graduate, if ever. People always need help with their sight. I can't tell a tension crack from a spider's thread without my glasses any more.'

Absurdly, Rodolfo found himself defending the very position he had repeatedly attacked in Ugo's seminars.

'You're confusing the etymology, Dad. The Latin prefix "semi" is derived from the Sanskrit *sami*, meaning a half or part, whereas semiotics is from the Greek *semeion*, a sign. It means the study of signs.'

'Like road signs?'

'Well, it's a bit more complex than that. Rightly considered, everything's a sign.'

There was a resonant thud.

'This isn't a sign. It's a damned table, for the love of God!'

Rodolfo instantly saw the massive scored and scorched surface, as though it were standing before him. But he had been trained by masters.

'In itself, it's nothing. Now that you've so designated it, then its signifier is indeed "a table" for the purposes of this text.'

'What do you mean, it's nothing?'

His father's voice had now taken on an edge of rage which Rodolfo found only too familiar.

'I built this bugger with my own hands from timbers I pulled out of the house where I was born! Hard, seasoned holm oak, at least four hundred years old. Christ, I could hardly cut or plane it even with the most powerful equipment. And you're telling me that it's nothing?'

'No word or other sign has any meaning except within the context of a specified discourse. That table is evidently laden with significance for you, given its physical sourcing in the construction material of your natal home, the notion of "the family board", and by extension the altar in church where communion is taken. But none of these intrinsically or necessarily adhere to the physical object you just struck. Surely that's obvious.'

His father sighed.

'All I know is that I built this table, and that my construction company now builds walls, bridges, roads, office blocks, apartment buildings, you name it. They either stay up or they fall down.'

'That's not the point. If someone says "This book's really good", they're not referring to an object that weighs so much and is such and such a size. They're talking about the text, the discourse, and the infinite variety of possible interpretations that it offers.'

'You and your damn books!'

There was a dry click as the receiver went down.

You and your damn books. Rodolfo surveyed the crowded shelves on his bedroom wall. Yeah well, they were going to have to go. Flavia too, for that matter. Might as well make a clean break. Apart from anything else, his father would go berserk if he learned that his only son had not only been expelled from university but was virtually living with an illegal immigrant from an eastern European country that no one had ever heard of, and whose real name almost certainly wasn't Flavia.

Which just left Ugo. Ideally he would have liked to draw a line there too, but couldn't imagine how it could be done. He began lifting the heavy volumes down and stacking them on the bedside table. As he pulled out Umberto Eco's *La struttura assente*, he noticed a dull metallic gleam peeking out from behind the next book on the shelf. He gazed at it for a moment, then reached in and removed a semi-automatic pistol. The wooden grip sported an elaborate metallic crest surmounted by a large red star, and the words 'Tony Speranza' were engraved on the barrel.

The door banged open and her supervisor walked in.

'So this is where you've been hiding!'

'I'm not hiding,' Flavia replied calmly. 'I'm putting away the equipment. My work is over.'

The balding gnome stared at her maliciously. He was sweating, and the array of pores on his nose resembled the backside of a bad cep. Conscious of the unearned superiority afforded by her looks and stature, Flavia felt a certain disinterested pity for him, although she would have killed him without a thought if the need had arisen.

'No it's not! The construction crew just finished putting up the set in B1, but everything's filthy, the event's at ten tomorrow morning and all the other girls have gone home.'

He put his head in his hands and sighed deeply.

'God, the day I've had! At the very last minute they decide to hold this stupid event, and guess who has to organise everything on less than twenty-four hours' notice? I managed to beg, borrow or steal the stoves, pans and all the rest of it from the exhibitors here, but then the stoves had to be hooked up and the whole fucking set constructed from scratch in less than eight hours. I've been going mad! Anyway, it's all done now, but the place is a total mess and we'll have the TV crew in here at crack of dawn tomorrow to set up. So get your illegal arse out there right now,' he snapped, stomping out, 'or I'll have it shipped back to wherever the hell it came from.'

Ruritania, she thought. I am the Princess Flavia, and mine is a Ruritanian arse.

She stacked her mop, pail, rags, bottles of cleanser and other equipment on to the trolley, and pushed it and the vacuum cleaner out into the vast arena, its ceiling festooned with an intricate mass of yellow piping like a giant molecular model. Another half-kilometre past stands displaying every kind of food, wine and kitchen equipment brought her to the double doors of hall B1. She shoved the door open with her Ruritanian arse, moved the gear inside and then turned to survey the extent of the task before her.

Any lingering feelings of self-pity and indignation instantly left her. The vast space was in darkness except for the brilliantly lit stage area, where two kitchens had been constructed, one on each side, with a fake dining room walled off between them. Flavia was instantly enchanted. It looked like a full-sized version of the doll's house she had played with as a child, before that and all the other family possessions, and indeed the family itself, had been dispersed. She had named it the House of Joy, and then transferred that epithet to the state orphanage to which she had later been sent, as if the concrete walls of that formidable institution could also be folded back and its roof lifted off to reveal a multitude of nooks and crannies where all manner of secrets could be kept accessible but safely out of sight. The memory of the books she had read so many times that she had them by heart, for example. As soon as she discovered the Italian text of one of them at a market stall in Trieste, she realised that it was a key that would unlock this odd dialect of her own sweet tongue. In the event, it had also served as the go-between in her introduction to Rodolfo.

It was, he had told her later, the first time he had ever set foot in La Carrozza, and he had only done so that evening because it had started pouring down with rain, and he was recovering from a bad cold. The arcades had protected him so far, but the next stage of his journey home was in the open and he would have got drenched to the skin if he had continued. Since there was nowhere else free, he had asked the young woman seated alone, who had finished her meal and was reading a book, if she would mind his joining her. The pizzeria was a no-nonsense establishment where questions like this were a mere polite formality, and Flavia had murmured agreement and waved to the empty chair without even looking up. Rodolfo had ordered some *olive ascolane* and a beer. Flavia was sitting over a cup of mediocre coffee, laboriously picking her way through the battered paperback garishly emblazoned with the title *Il Prigioniero di Zenda*.

'Excuse my asking,' the young man had said at length, 'but what are you reading?'

'I am learning Italian,' she'd replied. 'This is my textbook.'

He could easily have left it at that, or made some stupid remark which would have put an end to everything there and then. Instead, he nodded sagely, as though she had said something profound.

'Books are good, but to learn a language properly you really need a teacher.'

This had confused her, with its offered plethora of responses, but only for a moment.

'I can't afford such luxuries. Besides, I prefer to find things out by making mistakes.'

He had laughed, seemingly spontaneously, so that she forgave the impertinence of his next remark.

'God almighty, a woman who can make me laugh! Where have you been all my life?'

His name was of course already as familiar to her as her own, which perhaps helped to explain the ease with which things took their course, quite as though it had already been written in a book she knew by heart. But all books come to an end. Now, two months later, she sensed that the pack of unread pages was running low.

Never mind, there was work to be done. She walked out on

to the stage and set to work with a will, thinking about what she had overheard from another of the cleaning staff about what was to happen the next day. Some sort of duel, it seemed to be, like the one between Black Michael and King Rudolph's double, only with pots and pans instead of swords and pistols.

About ten minutes later a man and a woman came out on to the set from the wings, treading straight through the area that Flavia had just washed and waxed. She glared at them but said nothing.

'So, this is it,' the woman said to the man. She was about thirty, with fashionably distressed hair, was clad in a beige business suit and carried an imposing briefcase. 'This one will be your kitchen. Ugo's is on the other side. Both are visible to the audience, but not to each other or to the judges, who will be seated at the table in . . .'

'Delia!'

The man jogged her arm and pointed at Flavia. He was large and bearded, with the air of someone who would have liked to have a good time but didn't know how. That pushy crow he was with certainly wouldn't be able to help, thought Flavia, instinctively moved to take Lo Chef under her battered wings. Such scavengers had descended on her own country too, she had heard. Maybe Viorica had even become one. You needed serious wealth and clout to ship food parcels such as the one she had just received intact across so many frontiers.

The woman strode over to where Flavia was leaning on her mop.

'I'm sorry, but I must ask you to leave. I'm having a very important meeting with Signor Romano Rinaldi about his event tomorrow and we cannot be interrupted.'

Flavia shrugged.

'No capire. Di Ruritania.'

She waved her hand vaguely, as though indicating some

large but undefined shape at the rear of the set. Delia gave an irritable shake of the head and walked back to her companion.

'It's all right, she's just some asylum seeker. Doesn't understand Italian. Now, as I was saying, the jury will be in the central dining area through there, again visible to the audience but not to either of the competitors.'

The man took about half a dozen very short, very loud breaths. He grabbed a bottle of pills from his pocket and twisted the knob of a gleaming tap in the kitchen area. Nothing emerged.

'The water's not hooked up!' he squealed.

'It will be by tomorrow. Here, I've got some Ferrarelle.'

She passed him a plastic bottle and he downed the pills with a grimace.

'So, how many are ours?' he croaked.

'Paleotti, Aldrovandi, Sigonio, Colonna and Gentileschi,' Delia replied. 'Zappi and Giovio are leaning towards us, but could go either way, while Orsini will certainly vote for Ugo. They have the same publisher, apart from anything else. But that will just make it look better. The main thing is that whatever happens you're bound to win. So relax, okay? There's nothing to worry about.'

'That's easy for you to say! You're not the one who's going to have to stand up in front of Christ knows how many million viewers and actually do it.'

Flavia made a show of passing her mop over the false-tile vinyl floor, but in reality she was listening carefully. Her spoken Italian was not perfect as yet, although by no means as primitive as her reply to the crow had suggested, but she understood the language very well indeed. When you are a young woman, poor, powerless and alone in a strange land, you learn fast.

The woman called Delia gave a snort of what sounded like exasperation.

'Listen, Romano, everything's going to be all right. Trust me. You'll do fine, you'll look fabulous, and above all you'll clear your name of this ridiculous slur once and for all. If you're nervous, just double your normal dose of beta blockers.'

She paused and looked at him significantly.

'But nothing else, all right? No coke, no speed, and none of whatever those pills are that you've been popping. Not until the event's over. Understand? After that you can do what you like.'

The man nodded grudgingly. Delia indicated a large video screen hanging at an angle above the set.

'The list of ingredients will be displayed there. Glance at it briefly but with apparent interest. Remember, it's supposed to be the first time you've ever seen it. Scrutinise it with a nonchalant, relaxed expression, as if your mind is running through all the possibilities offered before making a spontaneous decision. Then turn decisively away, go to the stove and get the pasta water going before starting in on the sauce. Do everything with panache and *naturalezza*. Maybe sing a bit. But not too much, okay?'

She pointed to the kitchen counter.

'The ingredients will be laid out here. Just pick out the ones we've been through with Righi and leave the rest alone. No last-minute improvisation, please. I'll arrange for a litre bottle of *Lo Chef Che Canta e Incanta* oil to be placed here. Naturally a celebrity such as you wouldn't dream of using an inferior product, plus it'll give our label some nice exposure.'

She looked around.

'What else? Knives here, next to the cutting board. Pans over here. When the dish is ready, press this buzzer. Someone will come and take the pasta bowl from you and carry it out behind the set and in through the back of the dining area, so that in theory the jurors don't know which kitchen it came from. In fact your bowl has a distinctive orange patterning at the rim, subtly different from Ugo's. Our people will be in no doubt about which one is which.'

She looked at him.

'Any questions?'

'Something's going to go wrong,' the man replied in a dull voice. 'I just know it.'

'For God's sake, Romano! Nothing will go wrong. Nothing can. I've covered all the angles. All you have to do is be here on time, with a clear head, and put together a simple bowl of pasta that even I could make blindfold. Besides, it doesn't matter if it's any good or not. Haven't you understood yet? You're bound to win! It's all been arranged.'

She glanced at her watch.

'Right, let's go back to the hotel. The press conference starts in half an hour.'

When they had left, Flavia finished up her cleaning, then returned all the equipment to the storage room before leaving the concrete wasteland of the *fiera* complex and heading for the bus stop. The video display indicated that a smog alert was in effect, all vehicles with uneven numbered plates being banned from the streets, and that her bus would arrive in six minutes. She took out her phone and dialled.

'It's me. I had to work overtime because of this chef's duel they're having tomorrow. Where are you? Oh. Well, I'm starving. La Carrozza in half an hour? Yes, I know you're going through a bad patch, Rodolfo, but it will do you good to get out. Ah, here's my bus. *A presto, caro.*'

Flavia climbed aboard the bus with a smile on her lips that had nothing whatever to do with the silly intrigues on which she had been eavesdropping. I'm going to meet my prince, she thought.

Aurelio Zen's mind was wandering, and he was happy to let it do so. The air was acrid and savagely cold, the night starkly bright. On a frozen, floodlit field far below, men in suits and dark overcoats stood in line, heads bowed respectfully, awaiting their turn to step up to the podium and deliver a speech concerning the various virtues of Lorenzo Curti, their personal sense of loss and their perspectives on the unspeakable tragedy that his untimely death represented to everyone foregathered there, to the wider footballing community united at this moment in grief and remembrance, to the city of Bologna and indeed the nation and the world in general.

The surrounding environment consisted of concrete, steel and rows of blue plastic bucket seats which the spectators had lined with newspapers to protect their clothing from the residue of filth deposited there by the polluted void above. Apart from the amplified eulogies, the only sound was from the crowd of hardcore *ultra* fans at the far end of the stadium, who kept up a continuous low ululation, presumably a spontaneous expression of respect.

'I'll see you in the bar,' Zen told Bruno Nanni, getting up and starting along the narrow row between the seats towards the nearest aisle.

A total stranger whose foot Zen inadvertently stepped on looked up at him truculently.

'Leaving already? You might show a little respect.'

'I'm sorry,' Zen replied, shaking his head. 'I just can't take any more. It's like a death in the family. Do you understand?'

The man's expression changed to one of sympathy and he nodded.

Zen made his way through the cavernous vaults and vomitories of the stadium until he finally emerged in the bleak piazzetta outside, its scruffy grass borders and failed shrubs and trees exposed beneath the powerful and pitiless lighting ranged high overhead on steel poles.

On their arrival, Bruno had pointed out a bar in a neighbouring street as the unofficial clubhouse of the diehard Bologna supporters. At present the latter were still all inside the stadium, and the bar was almost empty. The most conspicuous figure was a bulky man wearing a double-breasted overcoat, a grey trilby and dark glasses. He was leaning casually against the rear wall, sipping a tumbler of whiskey and smoking an unfiltered American cigarette, and was fairly obviously a private detective. Apart from him, there were just three elderly men playing cards at the rear of the premises, and a woman of about their age who was sipping a glass of Fernet Branca and murmuring in a sustained monologue to a Pekinese dog that was a triumph of the taxidermist's art.

'... personally I want to be burnt when the time comes, even though it turns out you pay the same either way, well of course you don't pay but ...'

The ceiling was festooned with banners and flags in the team's red and blue colours, and the walls were covered in photographs of cup and league-winning squads dating back to well before World War Two. Zen ordered a coffee with a shot of grappa and took it over to a table.

Almost half an hour passed before the crowd started drifting out of the stadium. The bar soon filled up with young males wearing baseball caps, floppy jackets, even floppier pants, and synthetic sports shoes constructed along the lines of a club sandwich. They adopted a wide-legged stance, taking up as much room as possible, and loitered there with indefinite but vaguely menacing intent, talking and staring and drinking and twitching.

Feeling slightly overwhelmed, Zen stood up and found an elbow-level ledge against the mirror-clad pillar in the centre of the bar. The man dressed up as a private eye had now removed his shades and was gazing with intense concentration at a knot of particularly obnoxious newcomers who had taken up position to Zen's right. He kept bringing his right hand up to his face to inspect something in the palm, a mobile phone perhaps. The thought spurred Zen to check his own, which he had switched off in the stadium out of respect for the occasion. A text message appeared: *coming bo tomorrow lunch?* He hit the speed-dial buttons for the Lucca number, but there was no reply.

One of the fans came lurching back from the bar, a tall glass of some yellow liqueur in his hand. He was wearing a woolly hat, a black leather jacket with the club crest on the back, torn jeans and sports shoes, and walked straight into the mirrored pillar, spilling most of his drink over Zen's coat.

'*Cazzo!*' he spat out. 'Fuck you doing here, *vecchione*? Buy me another drink, you . . .'

But Zen had apparently been seized by a violent coughing attack, which caused him to lose his balance and lurch towards the younger man. A moment later the latter screamed and then collapsed on the tiled floor, just as Bruno appeared.

'He hit me!' the man on the floor yelled, thrashing wildly about. 'He kneed me in the fucking balls! Christ it hurts!'

All conversation in the bar ceased, but no one intervened. The complainant struggled painfully to his feet and turned on Bruno.

'You with him, Nanni?' he demanded aggressively.

Bruno nodded.

'So who is the old bastard?'

'A friend.'

There was a moment then when various things might have happened, then three of the man's companions came over and led him away.

'Sorry about that, *dottore*,' the patrolman remarked.

'He knows you, Bruno?'

Nanni shrugged.

'I'm not part of his tight set, but we all more or less know each other. The ones who go to away matches, I mean.'

'Does he know you're a policeman?'

'You think I'm crazy?'

He leant forward.

'Actually, he's the one I wanted you to meet.'

'The one who's bragging that he killed Curti?'

Bruno nodded.

'So who is he?'

'Name of Vincenzo Amadori. His father's a lawyer and his mother works for the regional government. One of the better families in town, as they say here. But the kid likes to act the desperate *emarginato* with nothing to lose. Comes on like he's one of the hardest cases at the stadium.'

'And the others accept him?'

Bruno shrugged.

'They tolerate him. Of course, it helps that he's got money. All the drinks tonight for that clique over there are on him, for example. He just hands the barman his credit card.'

'But he's not really liked?'

'I didn't notice anyone rushing to his aid just now.'

He looked wonderingly at Zen.

'Did you really knacker him?'

But Zen chose not to hear.

'Why is there nothing about any of this in the interim report on the Curti case?' he demanded.

Bruno dismissed the question with a wave.

'No one knows except me. In any case, it's just stadium gossip.'

'Or malicious misinformation put about by some rival gang of supporters who resent this Vincenzo Amadori's attitude and influence, and are trying to make trouble for him.'

'That's possible,' Bruno conceded. 'But there is one potentially substantive detail. That pack always hires a coach to take them to the away fixtures, so that they can travel together and stoke up on booze and God knows what before being shaken down by the cops at the entrance to the ground. I was rostered for duty the night Curti was shot, so I couldn't go to the game myself, but I've heard that Vincenzo travelled down to Ancona with the rest of them as usual, only when the coach left for the return trip he wasn't on it.'

Zen noticed the man in the trench coat and trilby heading for the door. He handed Bruno some money.

'Get us both a drink. A hot toddy for me And a damp cloth to clean this muck off my coat.'

'*Nervoso? Macché?* For me, the cooking is the life! I wait tomorrow like a promised spouse his moon of honey! Believe it, to be nervous, it is more the timorous adversary of me which is feeling himself in this mode! Ha, ha, ha, ha, ha!'

The Dutch journalist nodded in a mystified way and started muttering to his neighbour. Romano Rinaldi looked around the company with that trademark beaming smile, showing his very white teeth above the beard and generally radiating relaxed bonhomie. He could only stand another five minutes, he thought, catching Delia's eye meaningfully. She responded with a minimal vertical movement of her head, and Romano smiled even more largely and headed for the bathroom.

Safely locked in a cubicle, he took out one of the origami sachets stashed in his wallet and inhaled the contents off the back of his hand. Just the one, he thought, relishing the immediate, overwhelming rush of clarity and assurance. Well, maybe one more, what the hell. The main thing was that the evening was a success. More than that, a triumph! Everything was sparkling: the plates, the glasses, the lights, the company, and above all he himself, the star! He hadn't sampled the varied and delicious canapés the hotel had laid on, not having any appetite for anything but the crystalline powder – all right, one more line couldn't hurt – but this too fitted in perfectly, an act of genius demonstrating to the assembled contingent of foreign food pornographers that Romano Rinaldi disdained the products of even the best kitchen in Bologna. Nothing was good enough for Lo Chef but his own cooking.

The press conference had been hastily arranged with a view to promoting a version of his show abroad. The domestic market was pretty well saturated now, but there was a potentially vast audience elsewhere, above all the US. Italian food was hot. With his usual casual mastery, Romano had learnt to speak perfect English in a few months, as he had just demonstrated. The assembled journalists had clearly been astonished, even disconcerted, by his fluency. Most people in Europe understood at least some English, and if they didn't then they'd have to put up with subtitles or a voice-over. But the concept itself was solid, as he proceeded to explain in rapid Italian to the press corps when he floated back into the large private room that Delia had booked.

'For we Italians, cooking is not a thing apart. It is not just a skill or a trade, it is life itself! This is impossible for foreigners to understand. You people just eat something, anything, to stay alive, gobbling down your filthy meals like a bunch of neolithic savages in a cave! For we Italians it is very different. When we create *un piatto autentico, genuino e tipico*, it isn't just to satisfy our bodily hunger. No! We want to take inside ourselves all of Italy, her history, her culture, her language, her incomparable cities and landscapes. We want to imbibe the very heart and soul of this earthly paradise that is our native land! To you barbarians, food is a mere physical substance, so many calories and grams of fat, so much vitamin C and roughage. To us, this is a sacrilege! For we Italians, dining is like taking holy communion, tasting the very body and blood of our sacred culture that we consume in this daily domestic mass!'

Surrendering as always to the instinctive grasp of the public pulse that never deserted him, Rinaldi launched into a free adaptation of Verdi's '*Va, pensiero*'. Then he abruptly broke off in mid-phrase. His face darkened.

'Mind you, it hasn't always been easy for me. On the contrary! My enemies say I only do this for the money, the fame, the women, the fast cars, the jet-set lifestyle. And of course like every other talented and successful person in this country, I have many enemies. Only enemies, you might even say. They're all out to get me! You stupid foreigners visit Italy and think, "Beautiful villas, magnificent countryside, wonderful art, cooking and culture, a truly civilised country, an earthly paradise". You blind fools! You see only the pretty face and don't have the wit to realise that this stinking nation is nothing but a bloated corpse whose apparent signs of life only prove that the maggots are already heaving within! Paradise, my arse! Rather a Third World shithole inhabited by vicious, envious swine whose only thought is to try and drag me down to their own miserable level of insignificance!'

He breathed deeply for several seconds, then smiled at everyone seated around the table to indicate the utter futility of any such attempt.

'And now Professor Edgardo Ugo dares to suggest that I do not know how to cook! Ha, ha, ha, ha, ha! What does he know about Italian food and culture? He's spent so long locked up with his musty books that he's no better than you foreigners! Him, challenge me to prove myself? Don't make me laugh! He lives in an ivory tower, like all academics. He cares nothing for the *bel paese*, but me, I love it with all my body and soul. That's why I have dedicated my life to making the immortal masterpieces of our Italian cuisine accessible to the people, so that our long, proud and unbroken tradition may continue for many generations into the future!'

He burst into totally sincere tears. Several of the journalists began to gather their things together and eye the door.

'For him, it is all the head, not the heart!' Lo Chef continued, drying his eyes openly, unashamed of his worthy emotion. 'He is a thinker, but Romano Rinaldi is a lover! I COOK WITH MY COCK!!'

Delia had long since given up any attempt at translating this speech, and was now bustling around speaking to the departing journalists. Sensing the prevailing mood, Rinaldi switched effortlessly into his perfect English.

'Ugo dares quarrel me? Well! Soon he gets his want! This bastard say I know fuck nothing, but he is in error, my friends. Tomorrow I demonstrate once and for ever to you here, to my public, and to the entire world, that I know FUCK ALL!!!'

In the lobby, Rinaldi pressed the flesh assiduously, with Delia keeping a cautious eye on the proceedings.

'What I do now?' he replied to an unasked question. 'I walk! I inhale the air, I mingle with the people, I absorb the unique culture of Italy that lies all around, and I draw inspiration for the contest tomorrow. *Buona notte a tutti!*'

He walked out and up the street, turned several corners at random, then crossed Via Rizzoli, stepped up under the massive nineteenth-century arcade, ignoring the nasal whine of a crouched beggar, and strode in through a door beneath a neon sign depicting two golden arches.

'Give me a Big Tasty, a McRoyal Deluxe, a Crispy McBacon and five large fries,' he told the girl at the counter.

'Is that for here or to go?'

'To go, to go!'

'So apparently the whole thing's fixed! It's supposed to be a free-for-all followed by an impartial blind tasting, but the jury's been rigged. They'll know which bowl Lo Chef's stuff is in and then vote for it whatever it tastes like. So I'm afraid your Professor Ugo is bound to lose.'

Listening to Flavia chatter away, Rodolfo wished that he could enjoy his sense of power more. Killers were supposed to, by all accounts. That was what made it all worthwhile.

'He's going to lose all right.'

His doomed girlfriend had already devoured her entire pizza, including the crusts, and was now digging into a hefty slab of one of the *semifreddo* pies from the glass-fronted cooler near the door.

'Besides, Lo Chef has been told the list of ingredients in advance,' she went on, blithely unaware of her imminent fate. 'He's already chosen a recipe and practised it over and over again, just like my sister used to do with her piano test pieces at the conservatory. Mind you, there was always a sight unseen as well.'

Rodolfo looked up from the slice of pizza he had been morosely nibbling at for longer than it had taken to prepare.

'I didn't know your sister was a pianist,' he remarked in a stilted, stagey drawl. 'Does she have a thing?'

'I beg your pardon?'

'You know, a career. Sort of like a job, only more glam.'

Flavia finally displayed the first signs of sensing that something was wrong, although she couldn't of course have imagined in her wildest dreams that she was about to be shot through the heart.

'I don't know,' she replied guardedly. 'We've rather lost touch.'

'One always worries so much about these creative people. A gal's reach exceeding her grasp – or is it the other way around? Soaring dreams brought crashing down to earth, the inevitable brutal awakening to the harsh realities of life, and all that crap.'

Flavia made a moue he would have kissed, had it not been time to pull the trigger and have done.

'For my people, this is normal,' she said.

The waiter appeared with an unmarked litre bottle and two glasses, all frosty from the freezer. This was the home-made liqueur that was a speciality of La Carrozza, pure alcohol flavoured with a mixture of wild berries, lemon and spices, which was left on the table without appearing on the bill, a tradition of the house for regular customers. The upper two-thirds of the contents were a very light pinkish-purple, while the swamp of macerated berries occupied the lower section.

'Do you have any brothers or sisters?' Flavia asked. 'You never talk about your family.'

Rodolfo poured them both a drink, knocking his back to brace his nerves.

'Just a father. He phoned me today and we talked a lot, for the first time in ages. Maybe the first time ever.'

Flavia smiled warmly.

'That's nice. What did you talk about?'

'Failure. Professor Ugo expelled me from his course this morning. But I've decided that he unwittingly did me a favour. Failure's the key to everything. That's what these post-modern wankers don't realise, or won't accept. For them it's all relative. There's no such thing as failure, only alternative interpretations. It's all a state of mind. I believed that bullshit for a while myself, but now my eyes have been opened. I've definitely failed.

Shame about my academic career, shame about you, but that's the way it is. I just have a couple of things to take care of – this was one, by the way – and then I'm off home.'

Flavia sipped her drink.

'Ah, home,' she said, lighting a cigarette.

'Yes, but my home is a real place.'

Flavia drained the liqueur, immediately poured herself another and then lit a cigarette. She sat smoking in silence, looking all about the room at the other clients, the hefty *padrone* who made the pizzas, the two waiters who looked like that American silent film duo.

'I had to go to the university library today to return some overdue books,' Rodolfo said mechanically. 'I took the opportunity of consulting the index in the latest edition of the *Times* atlas. No Ruritania.'

He paused, still not meeting her eyes, but there was no response.

'So then I went to a computer terminal and did an online search. Apparently it's the name of a fictional country invented by some minor English writer as the locale for a trashy swashbuckling romance. The one you were reading when we first met, in fact. What you called your "Italian textbook". But the fact of the matter is that Ruritania doesn't exist.'

Flavia lowered her face to the filthy tablecloth as tears welled up in her eyes.

'It does exist! It does, it does, it does!'

Rodolfo smiled in a superior way and shrugged.

'If you say so. Of course, some people might say you were mad, but I prefer to assume that you've just been lying to me all along. And I don't care to be lied to.'

He placed some banknotes on the table.

'Well, I must be going. I've got a biggish day tomorrow. That'll cover the meal and a coffee, should you want one. *Addio*.'

The next morning, Aurelio Zen decided to raid the Amadori family residence. At least, this was how he jokingly put it to himself, over a coffee and the crispy, deep-fried batter wafers named *sfrappole*, in a bar on Via D'Azeglio almost opposite his hotel.

The breakfast buffet at the latter was an uninspiring concession to northern European businessmen visiting the city's famous trade fairs, who expected to start the day with a selection of cheeses, cold meats and hard-boiled eggs, washed down with watery coffee or tea. By contrast, Il Gran Bar was almost aggressively monocultural. The espresso was first-rate, and came with a complimentary glass of sparkling mineral water. The pastries were handmade and fresh, the waiters impeccably attentive, the clientele well-dressed and quietly spoken, but what was most striking were the decorative plaques and flags mounted on the walls, each bearing the emblem of a divisional unit of the anti-terrorist DIGOS squad and other elite units of the Polizia di Stato. In the context of historically 'red' Bologna, the message was clear: this was an unashamedly right-wing establishment in the rich 'black' area south of Piazza Nettuno, located comfortingly close to the central police station and the Prefettura, the bastions of state rather than local power.

Zen was of course an agent of that power, and had amused himself with the idea of using a little of it for the first time in months. After his visit to the football stadium with Bruno Nanni, he had spent a dreary and dispiriting evening alone – the first of many, no doubt – followed by a restless night during which he had skimmed through the written report on the

115

Curti case with which Salvatore Brunetti had fairly blatantly tried to fob him off. This had been made clear by the Bologna officer's remarks when they parted. 'I really must try and find time to look into the possibility of allocating you a suitable office, Dottor Zen. For the moment there just doesn't seem to be anything available. I do apologise, but your transfer here was very sudden. All leave has of course been cancelled and the entire staff is working three shifts around the clock, so the situation's a bit difficult. I hope you understand.'

Zen understood all right, and in normal circumstances would have been quite happy to stay well out of harm's way and keep his head down until the initial flurry of fuss about Curti had calmed down. But the circumstances were no longer normal, as he had been reminded, vividly and disturbingly, the night before. While going through his personal belongings in search of the generous selection of pills that he was supposed to take a varying number of times every twenty-four hours, he had discovered an envelope that the consultant had handed him on his visit to Rome, saying that the contents related to Zen's treatment and that he might find them 'of interest'.

Feeling that they might prove all too interesting in his current state of mind, or rather mindlessness, Zen had promptly forgotten the envelope until it turned up in a side pocket of the briefcase where he had packed his supply of drugs. In hopes of dispelling the vague fears that continued to haunt him, he had opened it and started to read the enclosed document, a technical report concerning his operation. This had been a mistake. Within moments, he felt himself reduced once again to the status of a helpless object, a piece of worn-out and much abused machinery consigned to the mechanics for short-term running repairs.

'. . . soft tissues were dissected away and the fascia was demonstrated on all sides of the necrotic tissue . . . a fine 11 blade was then used to incise the interface . . . and a site was selected distal to the area of involvement, the mesentery cleared adjacent to . . . which specimen was then presented to pathology . . . it was felt to be unwise to use mesh material for repair of the defect and . . . blood loss during the procedure was . . . the sponge count, needle count and instrument counts were correct and the patient tolerated the procedure quite well . . .'

The remainder of the night had passed miserably, and it was largely to try and regain a sense of initiative and competence that he formed the plan of visiting the Amadori family home. True, he had assured Salvatore Brunetti that he would be taking no active part in the Curti case, merely serving as an intermediary with the Ministry in Rome, but the detectives at the Questura were apparently not investigating the Vincenzo Amadori hypothesis – either because they didn't know about it, or had dismissed it as stadium tittle-tattle – so Zen felt justified in undertaking a modest preliminary investigation himself. Besides, one way or the other he had to escape from his pleasant but very small hotel room, its high ceiling freakishly out of proportion with the other dimensions owing to the intrapolated bathroom. This errand at least gave him a destination and the shadow of a pretext.

After breakfast, he walked down the street and out into the vacant, paved expanses of the city's main square, flanked by the uninspiring, red-brick mass of the cathedral towering above its unfinished marble facing, the modest but well-proportioned Palazzo del Podestà, the ornate Palazzo De'Banchi where luxury shops lurked beneath an imposing arcade, and the austere medieval façade of the Palazzo Communale, whose original delicate balance had been defaced by a monumental baroque excrescence erected in honour of one of the many popes who had sucked the city treasury dry over the centuries. There was nothing particularly wrong with any of this, but in his snobbish Venetian way Zen regarded it as not quite good enough. The enormous space seemed to make claims which the standard of the individual buildings couldn't justify.

The temperature was still below freezing, and he pushed briskly on into a warren of narrow streets that had obviously been the city's central food market for centuries. These were crowded with traders and their customers, mostly short, stout, elderly women enveloped in utilitarian fur coats from which their head and legs protruded as stubby appendages, giving them the appearance of so many furry pods. Zen's smugness instantly evaporated before the array of small shops to either side, displaying a dizzying selection of fruit, vegetables, cheeses and fresh meats infinitely more enticing than anything that either his native city or indeed Lucca had to offer. After weeks on a heavily restricted diet, the delights on offer had an almost sexually direct appeal, and made Zen impatient for lunch.

Fortunately the barrow-boy delivering cartons of Sicilian blood oranges to the kerb was strong, nimble, and had his wits about him, so when the *signore* who had been striding purposefully along the street suddenly stopped dead right in his path at the exact point where he was planning to set the heavy cart down, he was able to slew it to one side just far enough to prevent a collision that might otherwise have resulted in an interesting opportunity to compare the juice of the oranges with the liquid after which they were named.

Zen retreated rapidly with ritualistic apologies, but his mind was elsewhere. *'coming bo tomorrow lunch?'* He switched on his phone. There was no reply from their home number, but at the tenth tone Gemma answered her mobile.

'Can't talk now, we're just going into the hall.'

Her voice was a faint graffito scratched across a concrete wall of noise.

'I tried to call!' Zen hurled back. 'I tried several times, but there was no answer!'

He waited to be challenged about yet another egregious lie, but there was only the background babel. In reality, after that first attempt in the café outside the football stadium, he had never tried to contact Gemma about the message she had left him. He hadn't even remembered to neglect to do so.

'It's about to begin, I'll call you later,' he thought he might have heard someone say before hanging up.

The Amadori house, whose address Zen had earlier extracted from the Questura's records, was located in a quiet street west of the two medieval towers, one leaning at an alarming angle, that were among the city's most famous landmarks. The pavements here were raised about half a metre above the roadway, and protected from the elements by a set of infinitely varied yet harmonious *portici*. The house itself was of modest outward appearance, blending with grace and tact into the gently curving line of the whole block while nevertheless contributing its individual variation on the underlying architectural theme. It must have been worth well over a million euros.

Bruno Nanni had described the elder Amadori as a lawyer, and it was a very imprudent policeman who called uninvited on such a man without an excellent cover story, and preferably a judicial warrant. Zen had therefore planned his 'raid' carefully. There would of course be no mention of Lorenzo Curti, except as the subject of the memorial event at the football stadium the previous evening, following which Zen had been physically assaulted and verbally abused by a young man identified to him as Vincenzo Amadori. At this stage he had no wish to press charges or otherwise make an issue of the incident, but he considered it best that Vincenzo's parents should be informed so that they might take any action they considered appropriate. At the very least, it would be interesting to see what sort of reaction, or lack of it, he got to these allegations.

The front door was opened by a woman of about sixty, wary but unafraid, wearing a starched white blouse over a brassière resembling a major engineering project, a gingham pinafore and pink rubber gloves. Zen presented his police identification card and asked to see Dottor Amadori.

'*L'avvocato* is not here,' the woman replied.

'Do you happen to know when he'll be back?'

'I couldn't say, I'm sure. He's away on business. You'd need to ask at the office.'

'And *la signora*?'

'Also not at home.'

Zen smiled, pleasantly enough, but with just a hint of professional steeliness.

'To anyone? Or just to the police?'

The housemaid looked slightly affronted.

'What's this about?' she asked.

'A personal matter. I need to speak to a member of the family. What about the son, Vincenzo?'

A shake of the head.

'He doesn't live here any more.'

'Where does he live?'

The woman shrugged in a way suggesting that it was a mockery even to ask.

'Signora Amadori will be back in an hour or so.'

Zen nodded.

'Might I wait for her, do you think? It's a fairly routine matter, but we need to get it sorted out as soon as possible, and I'm a busy man. Since I'm already here . . .'

He gestured significantly. The maid hesitated a second, then opened the door fully and beckoned him across the threshold.

From the street, the house – like its guardian angel – had looked pleasingly plain and ordinary, with the subdued dignity of elderly people who no longer have anything they either can or need to prove. The interior, on the other hand, had been remodelled at some point in the late eighteenth or early nineteenth centuries, so that in entering one moved instantly but imperceptibly into a space not only mindful of its history and place in the greater scheme of things, but marginally more elegant and formal. The present owners had respected its simple, harmonious values, adding only a couple of inoffensive abstract oils in a now dated manner to the otherwise studiously neutral walls.

'This way, *signore*,' said the housemaid, peeling off her work gloves.

She led him up a steep stairway of marble steps with rounded edges flanked by elaborate wrought-iron banisters. The first-floor landing offered three doors. Zen was shown into what was obviously the formal *salotto*, at the front of the house, used on rare occasions as an impressive but impersonal 'receiving room'. It was large, with a ceiling even higher than the one in Zen's hutch at the hotel, and furnished with the type of 1970s 'contemporary' furniture designed to be admired rather than enjoyed. It was also bitterly cold.

'Would you care for a coffee?' the woman asked.

Zen reflected for a moment, and then gave her his warmest smile.

'That's very kind of you, *signora*. I'd love one, if it's not too much trouble. Would it be all right if I came down and had it with you in the kitchen?'

He laughed, as though in slight embarrassment.

'This room's a little chilly, and at my age . . .'

'Eh, the heating's always turned off in here, unless there are guests. Yes, of course, *signore*, come down. It's nothing grand

121

like this but you'll be nice and snug there, and I'll announce you as soon as Signora Amadori returns.'

They walked together to the stairs, which as Zen had noted on the way up were of old marble, heavily worn and polished to a lustrous sheen. He insisted that his companion go first, and about half-way down staged a carefully controlled fall backwards, accompanied by an impressive and convincing cry of pain.

The housemaid turned to him with horrified eyes.

'Jesus, Mary and Joseph!'

She came back up to where Zen lay and bent over him solicitously. He moaned and groaned a bit, then smiled and clambered unsteadily to his feet with the air of one bravely making light of a harrowing experience. Faking pain came easy after the crash course in the real thing that he had so recently undergone.

'Are you all right?' the *donna* cried.

'Nothing broken!' Zen replied, with a transparently faked if gallant attempt at jaunty humour. 'I'll be fine in a moment. But . . .'

He looked her in the eyes.

'What's your name, *signora*?'

'Carlotta.'

'Would you mind taking my arm as far as the bottom of the stairs, Carlotta?'

'Of course, of course!'

'It's disturbing, suddenly losing your balance like that. Makes you think about the day when you'll lose everything else too, eh?'

'Eh, eh!'

The two of them proceeded cautiously down, step by step. At the foot of the stairs, Zen did not withdraw his arm, nor did Carlotta release it. They shuffled back along the ground-floor passageway to a door at the far end that stood open into a dimly-lit, low-ceilinged area filled with odours and warmth. Leaving Zen to stand alone for a moment, Carlotta pulled over a chair and eased him into it.

'Now stay there,' she admonished him. 'I'm going to prepare a tonic. It'll make you feel much better.'

She bustled rapidly about the kitchen, opening cupboards, extracting containers, measuring ingredients, and then pouring, grinding and stirring. Carlotta's domain was evidently the one remaining original section of the house, saved by the cost factor – no need to impress the servants – from the upwardly-mobile renovations of some two centuries earlier. Although spotlessly clean, every surface looked worn, uneven, imperfect, and somehow denser than its actual physical consistency. The single fifty-watt bulb had no doubt been imposed by her employers for the same reasons of economy that had preserved the integrity of the whole space, but the gentle ingratiation of its dim glow, reflected back up off the worn flagstones, was beyond price.

'What's this?' Zen asked when Carlotta finally brought him a tumbler full of some brownish liquid.

'Just drink it down. All in one go, mind.'

He did so. Once the initial shock of the alcohol had subsided, he vaguely identified nutmeg, orange zest, cardamom and raw garlic. He nodded several times and handed the glass back, beaming at her.

'You're a wonder, Carlotta!'

'Now stay sitting where you are for five minutes, and you'll be as right as rain.'

She took the glass to the sink, shaking her head sorrowfully.

'I blame myself! To think that I'd polished those steps only five minutes before you arrived.'

'No, no, no!' Zen insisted. 'It was all my own fault, not looking where I was going. And these old leather-soled shoes are as smooth as . . .'

Their increasingly intimate colloquy – Zen was starting to think that he might well be able to get some interesting information out of Carlotta before he left – was interrupted by a dry, metallic snap in the resonant distance.

'That'll be the *signora*,' the maid declared. 'You stay here. I'll settle her down, then announce you as though you'd just arrived.'

She went out to the hallway, from which a duet of voices drifted back to where Zen sat idly waiting. Carlotta's he could recognise. The newcomer indeed sounded feminine, but there was a feeble, plaintive tone to the voice which ill suited the mental image he had formed of Signora Amadori. The words themselves were alternately ballooned and baffled as if by contrary winds, but they grew ever louder and closer until Carlotta reappeared in the kitchen, accompanied by a young man whom Zen didn't immediately recognise.

'Well, you should have told me!' the housemaid was saying. 'How was I supposed to know you'd had a nosebleed? I assumed it was a wine stain. If you'd told me it was blood then naturally I'd never have washed it in hot water, but how was I to know?'

'Why didn't you ask?'

'Don't you talk like that to me, Vincenzo! I've cleaned your nappies in my time, never mind your designer shirts. Take your precious stuff to a laundry if you're going to be so fussy.'

She broke off, realising that the young man had noted the police officer's presence, but seemed unable to come up with a satisfactory solution to this unforeseen social conundrum.

'What are you doing here?' Vincenzo demanded, advancing threateningly on Zen.

His intentions were clear enough, but his execution let him

down. His voice was still modulating from the plangent whine he had employed with the housekeeper to his peer-speak stadium bark, and when he reached the chair where Zen was seated he stopped short, seemingly uncertain how to follow through. Zen ignored him.

'That medicine of yours really did the trick,' he said to Carlotta, getting to his feet. 'I feel even better than when I arrived!'

Vincenzo swung round on the elderly *donna*.

'What's he doing here? What the fuck's going on?'

'You mind your tongue!' Carlotta fired back. 'Such language, and before a guest in your parents' house!'

Zen glanced at his watch.

'It's beginning to look as though Signora Amadori must have been delayed, and I've got other business to attend to. The matter's really of no urgency.'

'Just a moment, you!' Vincenzo shouted aggressively, although keeping his distance. Carlotta stood looking from one of them to the other, understandably out of her depth. Zen grinned at her roguishly.

'In fact, it might be better if you don't mention that I came at all,' he confided in a low voice. 'You know what lawyers are like. If Avvocato Amadori finds out that I fell on those slippery steps, he might lie awake at night worrying that I'm going to sue him.'

'Hey, you can't get out of it that easily . . .' Vincenzo began.

'As for you,' Zen cried, deigning to regard him for the first time, 'treat your mother with a little more respect!'

Vincenzo and Carlotta answered in chorus.

'She's not my mother!'

'He's not my son!'

Zen sighed, then shook his head in evident bafflement and walked out.

Gemma Santini reached the Bologna trade fair complex forty minutes before the event was due to begin, assuming that this would allow ample time to pick up her reserved ticket and get seated. She was wrong.

The area around the row of ticket booths was packed with people, some of whom gave every impression of having been there all night. Most were waiting their turn in a more or less orderly way for the strictly limited number of free passes being handed out to pack the hall, but a few had resorted to what Gemma privately called Neapolitan granny tactics, screaming their needs, demands and special circumstances at the attendant in the hope that they would be given what they wanted just to shut them up and get them out of there.

The moment she had learnt about the cook-off between her favourite TV personality and the awe-inspiring Edgardo Ugo which was to take place in the very city to which she was going anyway, her thoughts had turned to Luigi Piergentili. Although now a moral and physical wreck of the kind that dear Aurelio fondly imagined himself to be, in his former capacity as the dominant *consigliere* at the Monte dei Paschi bank Luigi had wielded a power in Tuscany and beyond second only to the equally fond imaginings of certain now-forgotten politicians. His own season of influence had been brought to an end – not entirely fortuitously, some held – by an unpleasant hit-and-run accident which had left the victim addicted, as he freely admitted, to a powerful morphine-based painkiller. Unfortunately, all of the many doctors he had consulted ultimately declined to continue prescribing this medication, citing normative pharmaceutical criteria, contra-indicative long-term health risks and, above all, a fear of losing their licences to practice medicine. It was at this point that Signor Piergentili had appealed to Gemma.

Luigi had been far too canny to make this appeal to her pity, or even her venality. Instead, with a shrewdness she had appreciated almost as much as the implicit *delicatezza*, he had murmured over tea at the Caffè di Simo that a very close friend of his, a professor at the University of Florence, had happened to mention to him that Gemma's son Stefano was studying engineering there.

'How is he doing?' he added, with a serene Etruscan smile.

The answer was spectacularly bad, but the smile made it clear that Luigi's friend had also mentioned that. Moments later, a mutually advantageous marriage of convenience had been arranged. Both parties had thus far remained faithful, but following Stefano's graduation *cum laude* Gemma, while duly grateful for the intercession concerned, had become the creditor in the relationship. She had therefore felt no qualms about phoning Luigi the day before, and telling him to work his network of contacts and fix her up with a comp ticket for the culinary showdown between Lo Chef and Il Professore. He had called back at dawn, after 'a blissfully dreamless night, thanks to you, my dear', with the news that she need only present herself at ticket counter 7 of the *fiera* compound in Bologna the next morning, and all would be taken care of.

This turned out to be true enough, as far as it went. What Gemma had not taken into account was the sheer crush of humanity attracted by this unique event. She didn't mind waiting, but like everyone else she was aware that since this event was being televised live, timing was of the essence. Once the broadcast began, the doors would be closed and locked, and even Luigi's pull wouldn't be able to get her in.

In the end, with a discreet elbow jab here, a piscine slither there, and a good deal of old-fashioned argy-bargy, she made it to the threshold of the hall with about a minute to spare, only for her mobile phone to go off. It was Aurelio, blathering away about something or other. She dealt with him very summarily and then processed into the arena with the other latecomers.

There must have been at least five hundred people present, Gemma estimated. Many of them wore identifying badges and name-tags on a cord round their necks, and busied themselves with tape-recorders, cameras and notebooks, but many were ordinary citizens who had queued up since dawn for a ticket to a contest that had been the talk of Italy ever since it had been announced. Her seat turned out to be a good one, about a third of the way up, with an excellent view of both kitchens and of the central dining area.

At ten o'clock precisely, the house lights went down and a man wearing shiny shoes, tight black trousers and a patterned silk shirt open to the navel, revealing a gold necklace nestling in his spectacular chest hair, stepped forward to the edge of the stage. With no particular surprise, other than the fact that he was so much smaller than she had imagined, Gemma recognised him as the presenter of a TV variety show broadcast on the same channel as *Lo Chef Che Canta e Incanta*. He proceeded to welcome the audience effusively, and then introduced the event and the participants in his usual bombastically jokey manner. Gemma noted, however, that once he got down to business the text of what he was evidently reading off a screen beneath one of the on-stage cameras had been very carefully scripted indeed, and almost certainly with a team of lawyers representing each party in the room.

In brief, it stated that Professor Edgardo Ugo, the noted Bolognese academic and world-famous author, had inadvertently written something in his column for *Il Prospetto* which might conceivably have been construed by the inattentive or ill-intentioned as casting doubt on Romano Rinaldi's culinary abilities. Such a thing had of course never remotely been Professor Ugo's intention. His comment had been made purely from a humorous and – the next word seemed to cause the presenter some trouble – metonymic perspective, and he unconditionally rejected any literal interpretation that might be placed on it. Nevertheless, to settle the matter once and for all, and also celebrate the glories of Italian cooking and the prestigious Bologna food fair, the two men would now 'meet as equal slaves over a hot stove [pause for laughter] before you all gathered here today and watching at home' in order to put a definitive end to any unpleasantness that might mistakenly have been perceived to have arisen.

'And now please welcome . . .'

The presenter gestured towards the kitchen area to the left of the stage as Edgardo Ugo walked in from the wings. The professor was wearing an English style tweed jacket, khaki cords, a rumpled dark-green shirt and a clashing lime-green tie, and looked as though he couldn't care less about the whole event. Acclaim from the audience was respectful but subdued.

'And in the opposite corner . . .'

Clad in his trademark white uniform and toque, Lo Chef made his appearance at a leisurely, relaxed pace, grinning confidently and waving to the crowd. The applause was tumultuous and so prolonged that after a considerable time the presenter was forced to appeal for silence.

The judges then filed in and were briefly introduced as leading chefs, cookery writers and culinary experts before taking their places at the dining table in the central section. After that the presenter began to explain the rules of engagement, and Gemma felt her interest slipping away. It was all about food, and she didn't feel in the least hungry, not least because it brought to mind Aurelio, whom she had unwisely contacted in a moment of elation the evening before with a virtual invitation to lunch and an implied reconciliation. She now felt very dubious about both, besides which she had been invited to dinner by Stefano and Lidia, who would be sure to take any lack of appetite on her part personally. Flicking idly through the brochure covering the Enogastexpo fair that she had been handed along with her pass, she noticed an advertisement for what sounded like a fashionable snack bar right in the centre, and texted Aurelio the name and address. That was the solution, she decided. A meaningless encounter, a quick bite, *e poi via*.

On stage, the presenter flung his arms wide, his expression one of astonishment and awe.

'And now, let battle commence!'

Gemma put the glossy brochure down and studied the two very different contestants. To the left, Edgardo Ugo had clearly resigned himself to his inevitable defeat. He sloped confusedly around his kitchen set under the brilliant TV lights in his pathetically homely garb like a parody of the drab, ineffectual bachelor wondering where everything was and what to do first.

Romano Rinaldi could not have presented a clearer contrast. From the very first moment, it was clear that he owned the space he had been allotted. He glanced at the display panel, then moved rapidly to turn up the flame under a pan of water for the pasta before turning his attentions to the ingredients and the chopping board. While Ugo pointedly ignored the onlookers and the cameras, turning his back all the time and never saying a word, Lo Chef romanced his audience constantly, chatting aloud, sharing his thoughts and cracking jokes.

Then he suddenly froze rigid for a long moment, as though struck by a spontaneous inspiration.

'*Ci vuole una cipolla!*' he proclaimed. 'I know it! How do I know it? Because the onion is calling out to me!'

Launching into '*Recondita armonia*', he sloshed copious quantities of his name-brand olive oil into a pan and set it on a high flame. The pasta water was now rising to the boil. Still singing and grinning, Rinaldi poured in the spaghetti and swirled it about a bit with a wooden spoon before seizing an onion from the array on the counter. He skinned and chopped it, then turned dramatically to the audience and walked downstage.

'The onion has spoken to me,' he said softly, wiping mock tears from his eyes. 'And what it has to say makes me weep.'

This provided an irresistible segue into Donizetti's '*Una furtiva lagrima*', during which the pot of pasta boiled over, flooding the right side of the stove and extinguishing the flame.

Rinaldi proved unable to relight the burner, despite hammering away repeatedly at the spark lighter function and then looking around in vain for matches. Meanwhile, on the other side of the stage, Edgardo Ugo was lumbering about like the caged bear he rather resembled, adding something to the sauce, keeping an eye on the pasta, and generally displaying complete indifference to whatever might be happening elsewhere. Eventually a businesslike woman of about thirty came running on to Rinaldi's kitchen set, moved the pasta pan to a different burner and ignited the flame before hastening offstage. Lo Chef turned to the audience, showing his teeth in a huge smile above his bearded chin.

'What a thing it is to have a woman around!' he declared in a tone at once humble and triumphant.

The audience burst into laughter and applause. Rinaldi acknowledged their appreciation of his wit and poise with a rendition of the famous aria from *Rigoletto*, changing the lyrics to '*La donna è mobile, ma indispensabile*'. This led to still more applause. Keenly in tune with the mood of his public, he proceeded with the rest of the piece, interpolating or altering lyrics as he went, before ending on a high and long-held note at the very edge of his vocal range.

It was at this moment that the pan of oil on the stove behind him burst into flames.

Tony Speranza made his way jauntily along Via Oberdan, a satisfied smile and a smouldering Camel on his lips. Passing a rather chic bar where he was known very well indeed, he turned in and ordered a double espresso and a whiskey. This fine establishment stocked not only Jack Daniels but also Maker's Mark, and on this occasion Tony decided to indulge himself with a large glass of the latter, even though designer bourbon was a little prissy for a true *investigatore privato*, strictly speaking.

But he had done the job, even if he hadn't yet been paid. This was becoming something of a sore point, particularly given the expense of replacing the miniaturised camera that had been stolen along with his beloved M-57 pistol back in Ancona. Nevertheless, he had got the photographs, which was the main thing. The digital shots of Vincenzo and his associates that Tony had taken in the café after the Curti memorial service the night before had been printed up on heavyweight A4 paper first thing that morning and delivered by hand to the client together with an itemised bill.

Actually his client had been out of the office when Tony called, but he had handed the sealed envelope, marked 'Urgent, Private and Personal', to a receptionist whose looks and manner suggested that her rates would put a high-class hooker to shame, with instructions to hand it to *l'avvocato* immediately on his return. For form's sake, he had then flirted a bit with the leggy lovely, who had coyly pretended to be interested only in her work, before returning to the mean streets.

After lunch he would phone Amadori senior and press for immediate payment of the fee they had agreed, as well as his substantial expenses to date, including of course the Maker's Mark, of which he ordered another glass. In short, everything was great, except for the gnawing sense of existential emptiness that always came over him once a case was closed. How much longer before the day came, as he knew it must, when the moral and physical strain became too much to bear? Tony had been a gumshoe for over twenty years now, ever since the day he was dismissed from the police force after shooting two passers-by while failing to arrest a sneak thief who had fled with a pocketful of discount coupons after holding up one of the cashiers in a Conad grocery store. Twenty years was a long time in this filthy trade.

He knocked back the second bourbon and lit another Camel. Hell, he was good for another twenty, as long as his luck held and he didn't stop a shell from some punk in a speakeasy down by the docks. Actually there weren't any docks in Bologna, but one of his cases might take him down the road to Ravenna some day. Now there was one tough town. But that was the way it was with this stinking job. You never knew what was coming your way next, except that it wouldn't be good news.

As if to demonstrate this, he caught sight of something in the big mirror at the rear of the bar, which reflected the front window and the street beyond. He threw some cash at the barman and hustled out. There, about ten metres away, was the unmistakable battered black leather jacket bearing the crest of the Bologna football club on the back. Tony began to follow circumspectly. It was good to see that Vincenzo had started wearing the bugged garment on occasions other than his visits to the stadium. That would make life so much easier if *l'avvocato* decided to hire Tony for the long-term maintenance service that he always recommended to his clients in the interests of their continuing peace of mind.

134

The man in front turned left and cut through the side streets to Via Zamboni, Tony keeping a constant ten metres back. Then it was left again, past the church of San Giacomo and the theatre to the university, where the subject ran up the steps and into the main building. At this, Tony shrugged and turned back. He couldn't possibly keep up a covert tail in that maze of corridors packed with people half his age. What was the point, anyway? Apparently Vincenzo Amadori had decided to start studying again. Fine. That would be some good news that Tony could use to sweeten the pill when he called the kid's father to demand his money, while the fact that he was aware of it provided conclusive proof that he was tirelessly on the job, fulfilling his promise to provide the assurance of knowing everything, always!

'When I speak of mimicking mimesis, an exact parallel is to be found in contemporary cosmology, where there is much discussion about the problem of the apparent "fine-tuning" of our observable universe. Since any appeal to a divine author, with an independent existence *hors du texte*, is clearly out of the question, scientists have advanced and indeed largely accepted the so-called multiverse or "all possible worlds" theory. This postulates an infinite number of parallel universes exhausting every conceivable permutation of the physical constants. It is thus unsurprising that we happen to find ourselves in the statistically insignificant instance where those constants are such as to make human life possible. This is the only universe that we can experience, but in order to make sense of its apparently purposeful calibration we must – I repeat, must – presume the existence of all possible variants, since any other outcome is a nonsense a priori.

'By analogy, each text necessarily implies the existence of an infinite number of other and in many cases contradictory texts. Over a century ago, Nietzsche proclaimed that "There is no such thing as facts, only interpretation". In one or another parallel universe, Noam Chomsky's notorious example of a grammatically correct yet semantically meaningless statement, "Colourless green ideas sleep furiously", would sound as banal as "The cat sat on the mat". Hence the inherent instability of any given interpretation, despite the competing claims of the various class, power and gender structures that it might appear to endorse.'

The lecture hall was a classic seventeenth-century *aula* resembling the theatres and opera houses of that period:

chaste, intimate, and with perfect acoustics. Professor Edgardo Ugo's conversational voice carried, without any effort or amplification, to the seat high in the back row where Rodolfo Mattioli sat. He knew that he would be invisible to Ugo from there, but he was in any case wearing Vincenzo's scuffed leather jacket once again, this time to avoid recognition.

Professor Ego, as he was known to students and fellow academics alike, had now reached his peroration. Characteristically, this combined witty and learned references to Eugenio Montale, the video game *Final Fantasy X-2*, Roman Jakobson, the Schrödinger's cat paradox, St Thomas Aquinas, *Invasion of the Body Snatchers*, transcendental number theory and the Baghdad blogger. He then accepted the plaudits of his audience with an equally characteristic gesture indicating that while he understood, as they of course did, that none of this was of any real importance, they also understood that nothing else was either. Or as Ugo liked to put it, adapting Oscar Wilde, 'We are all in the gutter, but some of us no longer pretend to be looking at the stars'.

Rodolfo filed out with the rest of the auditors, several of whom glanced at him with embarrassment, and then looked away. The news of his expulsion from Ugo's course had clearly got around the other students involved. He was now taboo. If only they knew, he thought, fingering the pistol pocketed in the leather jacket. The previous evening Rodolfo had extracted and carefully examined the weapon he had discovered concealed behind the books in his room. It was a very high-quality piece of hardware, of Soviet origin judging by the red star on the grip, and to all appearances brand-new, but a faint odour of cordite in the barrel and the fact that there were only seven cartridges in the magazine, which was designed to hold eight, suggested that it had been fired at least once.

Rodolfo was no novice when it came to guns. On his arduous ascent through the lower echelons of the post-war construction business in Puglia, his father had been obliged to learn how to maintain and use a variety of firearms. He had passed this knowledge on to Rodolfo as a father-son bonding exercise, taking the boy out into the wilds from their country property for target practice. He had graduated from cans and bottles to vermin and birds, and in hopes of pleasing his father had developed into quite an accomplished shooter.

Well, today he was going to put those long-neglected skills to the test. He walked down the corridor and staircases with the rest of the student throng, amusing himself abstractly with the thought that at any moment he could kill seven of them. That wasn't going to happen, of course. Apart from anything else, the random, motiveless crime was so last century, one of the great clichés of modernism both artistically and politically. Someone like Vincenzo, who hadn't realised that the only stars he could see were the flashes in his head as a result of collapsing in the gutter, might still get a kick out of that sort of thing, but not Rodolfo. His *acte* was not going to be *gratuite* so much as *in omaggio*. His gestural rhetoric would be flawless, and then he would catch the first southbound train, turn up on the family doorstep at dawn, admit his academic disgrace and humiliation and beg his father to give him a real job.

After his weekly lecture, Rodolfo knew, Edgardo Ugo left the building by a side door leading to the bicycle shed reserved for the faculty. There the professor retrieved his machine and cycled the short distance to his town house to relax and prepare for lunch. Rodolfo therefore posted himself at the gate leading from this area to the main street. He himself didn't have a bicycle, but he had noted in the past that, in keeping with the traditions of his city, Ugo proceeded on two wheels at a civilised, leisurely pace barely faster than a brisk jog. What with the inevitable traffic delays, Rodolfo had no doubts about his ability to keep up with his quarry for the kilometre or so separating the university from Ugo's bijou residence in Via dell'Inferno. And there, he thought to himself, remembering Vincenzo's taunting remark, I'll give the smug bastard something to interpret.

Gasping in pain, he lurched to his feet, overturning the row of stools like so many dominoes, and ripped open his shirt. Beneath the violated fabric of his belly, mighty worms stirred. The flesh glowed incandescently red and yellow, casting into black outline the scalpel scar curved like a question mark about his navel. Then the overstrained sutures finally unclasped, releasing a scalding discharge of foul-smelling pus and blood that drenched the other diners, all of whom carried on eating and chatting as if nothing at all had happened, which in fact it hadn't.

'*Caffè, liquore?*' enquired the waiter.

Zen shook his head peremptorily. There was a sudden burst of laughter and one of the people perched at the counter near by pointed to the huge flat-screen television displaying images of a bearded man dressed as a chef running wildly about in a kitchen on fire. The dangling TV was all of a piece with the high concept behind the eatery, in effect a very pricey snack bar with deliberately uncomfortable furniture, a selection of wines by the glass at by-the-bottle prices, and patrons who apparently relished colluding with the staff in creating a spuriously sophisticated atmosphere of mutual disdain. All this tucked away on a narrow cobbled street that went nowhere in particular, with a frontage that was diffident in the extreme. Not for the first time, Zen reflected that while prostitution might be the oldest trade in the world, the catering business ran it a close second, and that there were other similarities.

But none of this was of any importance compared with the fact that he was still alone. Well over an hour now, and no sign of Gemma. He had tried repeatedly calling her mobile, but either the battery had run out or it was switched off. After waiting thirty minutes, he had ordered the dish of the day – he couldn't even remember now what it had been – and eaten it with a morose appetite. He checked her text message again. There it was, the name and address of this ghastly place, even the phone number. Impossible there could be any mistake. Anyway, she had the number of his mobile, which he had left turned on all this time. The only possible conclusion, therefore, was that she had deliberately stood him up. He hadn't expected anything quite so crude from Gemma, even at her worst, but there it was.

He had already asked for his bill when the door opened and in she walked, wearing a stylish but rather stern outfit. Her face, by contrast, was flushed and open, and her manner bubbling with barely suppressed hilarity.

'Sorry I'm late,' she cried, collapsing at the table and lighting a cigarette. 'You'll never guess what happened! Or did you see it?'

She burst into laughter, which turned to a long series of coughs, during which the supercilious waiter appeared.

'Nothing, thanks,' she said, waving him away.

'You don't want to eat?' asked Zen.

'I grabbed a *panino* at a bar near the exhibition grounds while I was waiting. There wasn't a taxi to be had for ages, of course.'

She erupted with laughter again.

'Did you see what happened?'

Zen stared at her, still half-suspecting a trap, but her defences were clearly down. The only problem was that he still had no idea what she was talking about.

'See? Where?'

'On TV.'

Gemma pointed to the screen, now showing the President of

the Republic inspecting a guard of honour in the quaintly ornate capital of some eastern European state which had recently come in from the cold war.

'*Caffè, liquore?'* enquired the waiter, surfacing again with such animus that they both relented to the extent of ordering coffees.

'You have no idea what I'm talking about, have you?' said Gemma, laughing again. 'You must be the only person in the country who doesn't!'

She reached over and touched Zen's wrist on the tabletop, only for a moment, but enough to set off another of the intestinal twinges which reminded him again of that scene from a science fiction film they had once rented on video, where one of the crew of a spaceship discovers in the most unpleasant way that an alien parasite is nesting in his innards.

'You know that TV show you hate?' she went on blithely. '*Lo Chef Che Canta e Incanta*? Well, I'd heard that the star was going to be performing live today at the food fair that's on here, so I naturally took advantage, seeing that I was coming up anyway.'

Zen nodded.

'To see me,' he murmured.

Gemma's expression blurred for a moment.

'Well, actually Stefano asked me to come up over the weekend. Some domestic business he wants to discuss. You know about him and Lidia, right? They're living here in Bologna and apparently something has happened. I'm pretty sure I can guess what it is, but of course they want to make a big fuss about it, and rightly so. Anyway, it meant I could see you, and also drop in on this *mano a mano* between Rinaldi and Ugo. Of course no one thought that it would be any contest. I mean, the biggest celebrity chef in the country up against a total amateur!'

She laughed, throwing back her head and revealing her beautiful throat.

'Well, guess what? It was indeed no contest, because the contest never took place!'

Their coffees were gracelessly delivered. Zen slurped his, lit a cigarette, and tried his best to enter into the spirit of whatever this was.

'Did one of them cancel at the last minute?' he asked.

'Much better than that. Or worse. Ugo just pottered around his kitchen, getting on with the job and not making a fuss about it. In fact I sort of liked him. He looked all sweet and cuddly and a bit incompetent, not at all what I'd imagined from trying to read that impossible novel that everyone bought and then pretended they'd read. In fact I wouldn't mind running into him while I'm here in Bologna.'

'I don't imagine there's much chance of that.'

'Of course not, but a girl can dream. Anyway, over on the other side of the stage, Lo Chef was doing his usual act, all very dramatic and "look at me", chatting up the audience the whole time and then breaking into some fake operatic aria. Unfortunately he gets so carried away that he forgets he has left a pan full of oil on the stove, and right in the middle of one of his big numbers it goes up in flames! The set itself was obviously cobbled together at the last minute from flimsy wooden panels and they're ablaze before anyone can do anything about it. Next thing, the auditorium is filled with smoke, fire alarms are going off everywhere and the whole place has to be evacuated. And I mean the whole *fiera* site, the entire Enogastexpo show! Thousands of people milling around in the car parks, the fire engines pouring in, police helicopters overhead, utter chaos!'

Zen let a few moments elapse before saying, 'So tonight you're seeing your son and his . . .'

'Yes.'

'What's that about?'

Gemma looked at him with a slightly coy smile.

'Well, Stefano didn't want to say on the phone, but I have a feeling that I may be going to become a grandmother.'

Zen grazed on this thought for some time.

'Which would make me . . .' he finally began.

'Nothing.'

They confronted each other for a moment over this.

'Nothing at all,' said Gemma in a harder voice. 'We're not married, and for that matter neither are they. So it's of no consequence at all, really. To you, at least.'

Zen tried to think of something suitable to say.

'Are you staying the night?' he managed at last.

Gemma shook her head.

'They can't put me up. It's just a one-bedroom apartment that her parents are letting them use.'

Zen gave her the look he often used on a suspect who had just revealed more than he knew.

'So she wears the trousers,' he said.

Another moment of confrontation.

'They're a couple,' Gemma said very distinctly, as though speaking to a foreigner with a limited understanding of the language.

'But she's in charge,' Zen insisted.

'I wouldn't know.'

'She owns the house, *cara*. Just like you.'

Their eyes met, and he instantly realised that he'd gone too far. A moment later he felt another pang in his gut and saw a chance to lighten the mood.

'Get out!' he ordered the imaginary resident alien with an exaggerated gruffness that was intended to be comic. 'Get out, get out!'

But Gemma had forgotten the movie involved in this reference and couldn't have been expected to understand the connection anyway. Assuming that Zen was addressing her, she
sprang to her feet and ran to the door.

Edgardo Ugo was cycling home, when something happened.

He was feeling serene and light-hearted, totally at ease with himself, with the city he knew so well and loved so much, and with life in general. To his utter amazement, he had scored an incontrovertible triumph in the much-publicised contest with Rinaldi. Admittedly this had been due to the other man's unbelievable incompetence, but the result had been no less conclusive. Let the bastard try and sue him now! After that, refusing to comment on the proceedings to the throng of journalists clustered outside the evacuated exhibition centre, he had taken a cab straight to the university and delivered his famous weekly lecture with his usual calm professionalism, as though he'd just returned from a visit to the library.

Now he was heading back to the little urban *pied-à-terre* that he maintained a short distance from the university, to freshen up and change out of his smoke-poisoned clothes before going to lunch with a visiting academic from the University of Uppsala. By bicycle, of course. In Bologna, bicycles were associated with the populace: impoverished students, pensioners scraping by, penny-pinching housewives and the like. For a world-famous author and academic, with untold millions in the bank, to be seen on one instantly transformed his battered though structurally handsome 1923 Bianchi S24 from a humble means of transport into what semioticians called a 'sign vehicle', thus making one of those arcane jokes for which Ugo was famous. God, he was cool.

And then something happened.

Afterwards, of course, it was perfectly obvious what this was, but the instant offered nothing but fleeting and confused impressions, followed by a sickening loss of balance, the jar-ring impact, and multiple aches and pains. The next thing he was distinctly aware of was a man standing over him. Ugo himself appeared to be lying on the cobbled street with the handlebar of the bicycle lodged somewhere in his kidneys.

'Aurelio Zen, Polizia di Stato,' the man snapped, displaying some sort of identification card. 'You're under arrest for dangerous driving.'

Ugo tried to say something, but the man had turned away and was loudly phoning for an ambulance. It was then that Ugo saw a woman leaning groggily against the nearest parked car. There was blood on her face and she was breathing rapidly.

'Immediately!' the policeman named Zen yelled. 'It's a matter of the highest urgency. My wife has been run over.'

'I'm not your damned wife!' the woman retorted.

The man folded up his mobile and strode over to Ugo, who had by now regained his feet. He looked absolutely beside himself with fury, or worry, or both.

'I can't effect an arrest now,' the policeman told him, 'as I need to accompany the victim to hospital. But if she turns out to be seriously injured, God forbid, then I shall take further steps. Give me your details.'

Ugo got out his wallet and handed Zen his identity card, along with another giving his home address and title, position and contact numbers at the university. That might get him a little respect, he thought, picking up his bike as a siren made itself heard in the distance.

'Excuse me!'

He turned. The woman he had struck was looking at him.

'Aren't you Edgardo Ugo?'

He nodded. She smiled and her bloodied face lit up.

'I've always wanted to meet you,' she went on. 'I was at

your cook-off with Lo Chef this morning. I thought you were wonderful!'

For possibly the first time in his life, Edgardo Ugo found himself at a complete loss for words.

'I'm so sorry that this happened,' he said at last. 'I can't apologise enough.'

The woman laughed lightly.

'Not at all, it was all my fault.' She jerked a thumb at Zen, who was anxiously scanning the far end of the street for the ambulance. 'We just had a row and I couldn't get away from the restaurant quickly enough. I dashed out without even looking to see what was coming. There was no way you could have done anything about it.'

'Here it comes!' called Zen.

'And don't pay any attention to him,' Gemma confided to Ugo. 'All that stuff about arresting you? That's just bluff and bluster.'

Then the ambulance was there, the paramedics stepping out. Ugo mounted the Bianchi and tried to cycle discreetly away, but the collision had dislodged the drive chain. He didn't want to get his fingers filthy, or to linger, so he set off on foot, pushing the bike.

At the corner of the street, beneath the arch marking the entrance to the former ghetto, he turned to look back. Apparently the ambulance crew didn't consider the woman's condition serious enough to put her on a stretcher and were getting her seated in the back of the ambulance. The incident had drawn quite a crowd, including one young man wearing a black leather jacket decorated with the crest of the local foot-ball club. He also noticed that the policeman who had threat-ened him did not in fact get into the ambulance, as he had said he would, but watched it depart, then turned and started walking in Ugo's direction.

Ugo turned the corner with a shrug. If the cop wanted to find him, he had the address anyway. Meanwhile he marvelled at the day's extraordinary events. To knock someone down in the street and then have her tell you how wonderful you were! Incredible. He just hoped that she wasn't concussed. Anyway, that was enough excitement. A hot shower and a change of clothes, then off to a leisurely late lunch with Professor Erik Lönnrot. He leant the bicycle against the house wall, between the front door and the marble copy of Marcel Duchamp's 1917 ready-made *Fountain*. He found his key and turned sideways to force it into the sticky lock.

And then something else happened.

Romano Rinaldi paced restlessly and at random through the many rooms of his hotel suite, a continual gyration with no purpose except to relieve the intolerable pressure in his skull. He knew, beyond the slightest doubt, that he was going to die at any moment. What was it called? An aneurysm, a stroke, a cerebral haemorrhage. Basically your brain blew up.

He walked through to the main bedroom, then over to the insulated glass doors giving on to the balcony over the street. The temptation to gasp down some fresh air was almost over-whelming, but he couldn't risk showing himself, not with the ranks of paparazzi lined up like a firing squad detail below, fingers hovering over the shutter release for the front cover 'HIS SHAME' shot. Instead it was through into the spare bed-room and then down the internal hall to the lounge that stretched the entire width of the building. Despite his best efforts, he could hardly avoid catching sight of himself in the vast mirror that dominated the end wall.

I'm fucked, he thought, staring at his sagging features, totally and utterly fucked. And it's all my own fault. It was mine to leave alone, but I agreed to take it on. After that it was mine to screw up, and I did just that, in front of an audience of mil-lions. The TV news channels would show the highlights again and again and again, until the whole country had witnessed his utter humiliation. He would be laughed at in the street and people would snigger when he was introduced to them. As for his career as *Lo Chef Che Canta e Incanta*, forget it. He would be carrying his shame about with him for the rest of his life, like those dogs you saw with a plastic bag of their own shit hang-ing from their collars.

He clutched his head and stared in the mirror. That prominent vein on his temple was surely even more engorged than it had been five minutes ago. Get Delia to call an ambulance. There had been good hospitals in Bologna ever since the Middle Ages. Back then they let blood to relieve the pressure. Leeches. That obscene object he'd been offered in a bento box when he visited Tokyo last year, some sort of raw snail out of its shell. An elegantly lacquered casket with a skinned penis inside. Well, after this he wouldn't be invited to any more international culinary conferences, that was for sure.

On leaving the *fiera* complex – fortunately his production company had laid on a car in the VIP section of the parking lot, so he hadn't had to face the mob outside the main entrance – Rinaldi had gone straight back to his hotel, entering through the kitchens, where his sudden appearance had generated a good deal of mirth and sight gags involving fire extinguishers among the lagered-up, sweated-out peons. Then up the emergency stairs to his suite, where he had double-locked and chained the door, taken the phone off the hook and switched off his mobile before snorting his entire remaining stash of cocaine. Unfortunately there hadn't been that much left, and by now the effects had worn off. He switched the mobile on again, ignoring the backlog of messages, and dialled Delia.

'Bring me two bottles of vodka and a bucket of ice,' he said, cutting off the speech into which she immediately launched. 'Personally. Now.'

Five minutes later there was a timid tap at the door. Rinaldi peeked through the spy-hole and verified that it was indeed Delia, and that she was alone, before dismantling his barricade and letting her in.

'Put it down there,' he said, pointing to the floor of the entrance hall.

But Delia kept going straight into the lounge, where she

deposited the two bottles and the silver bucket on a glass-topped table.

'Get out of here!' Rinaldi shouted, coming after her. 'I need to be alone.'

'We have to talk, Romano.'

'There's nothing to talk about.'

Delia sank into a sofa the size of an average family car.

'*Carissimo*, I've been trying to call you for hours!'

Rinaldi dropped four large ice cubes into a tall tumbler, filled it to the brink with vodka, and drank deeply.

'Why didn't you answer my messages?' Delia went on in an irritating, deep-down-inside-I'm-just-a little-girl whine. 'How can I help you if you won't even speak to me?'

'Nobody can help me. And I can't help your career along any more, so don't pretend to be personally interested. It's over. Me, you, the series, the company, everything.'

'That's absurd, Romano! You can't just chuck the whole thing away because of a silly accident.'

He gulped some more vodka and almost choked as he burst into incredulous laughter.

'Silly accident! I almost burnt down the Bologna exhibition centre! For all I know the police are after me.'

'It wasn't your fault! How were you to know that the dial controlling the burners on the stove hadn't been calibrated properly? All the kitchen equipment was rounded up at the last moment from the manufacturers exhibiting at Enogastexpo. They have a few functional demonstration models, but most of the hardware is on static display. It was one of those units that was placed in your kitchen area. The fitters connected it to the gas supply, but they didn't have time to fine-tune all the various functions. So you put that pan of oil on over what you thought was low heat, then turned away to do other things and entertain your fans. In fact, the flame under the pan was hotter than the safety regulations allow for that kind of stove even at the very highest setting! The outcome was inevitable.'

Rinaldi finished his drink and immediately poured another.

'No one will believe that.'

Delia got to her feet and eyed him levelly.

'They will when the managing director of the company that manufactured the stove confirms it tomorrow morning, having conducted a personal examination of the unit in question.'

A contemptuous shrug.

'Why should he want to help?'

'Well now, I wonder. Maybe the hundred thousand from the broadcasters had something to do with it.'

Rinaldi stared at her in wonderment.

'They've bribed him?'

'Of course they have. You're one of their premium products for the foreseeable future, Romano. They aren't going to give you up without a fight.'

She came over and stood very close to him, looking him unblinkingly in the eyes.

'All you have to do is keep your head down for the next few days. No interviews, no comments, no phone calls except to and from me. In fact it would be best if you didn't even appear in public. Why don't you just stay here?'

Rinaldi shook his head violently.

'Out of the question!'

Apart from anything else, he couldn't possibly show his face in any restaurant in town, where most of the clients would be attending the Enogastexpo. Even room service would be risky. 'Sorry, sir, Bologna fire regulations prohibit the preparation of flambéed dishes in the rooms, heh heh heh.'

Delia nodded.

'In that case, we go to Plan B. One of the directors of our TV channel owns a villa in Umbria. It's luxurious and very remote. At seven this evening I'll have a car waiting for you at the back door of the hotel to whisk you off. There'll be a well-stocked larder and cocktail cabinet, not to mention a selection of your favourite recreational drugs. When everything's pre-pared, we'll bring you down to Rome for a well-rehearsed press conference. You'll have been coached with an answer to every conceivable question. Then, at the end, you publicly challenge Edgardo Ugo to a replay.'

Rinaldi jolted so violently he spilled most of his drink.

'Go through that again? Are you crazy?'

Delia laid her hand on his arm.

'You won't have to, Romano. Ugo's lawyer is already in pos-session of a document guaranteeing that we will not pursue any claims against his client regardless of the result of today's contest. Ugo has nothing left to gain, so he will decline our offer. But you will have made it, which makes you look good. After that it's back to business as usual, planning the summer series of the show. *Va bene?*'

Rinaldi thought this over for some time. Actually it didn't sound too bad. Maybe there was hope after all.

'Va bene.'

He saw Delia to the door, and bolted and chained it after her. Back in the lounge, he replenished his glass and started to wander about again, but at a more relaxed pace than before. Vodka was good stuff, taken in sufficient quantities, but after the day he'd had Rinaldi reckoned that he deserved some of the very best. He wouldn't be able to get that here, of course, but even a relatively modest product would be better than nothing. Once it got dark and the press corps gave up, he would slip out and try asking in a few bars around the univer-sity area. It never hurt to ask.

The moment the automatic doors of the Policlinico Sant'Orsola swished to behind him, Zen felt at home. It was good to be back in that calm, purposeful, well-ordered world, where an atmosphere of assured competence prevailed and questions of life and death were discussed in cool, measured undertones. Of course, it wasn't like that in Palermo or Naples – or even Rome, which is why Zen had gone to a private clinic – but the high civic values of the Bolognese ensured that their public hospital was a model of its kind.

Nevertheless, the lowly and marginal status of non-patient, lacking the talismanic plastic wrist-strap, meant that passing through the various internal frontiers took a lot longer. Zen's police identity card helped to an extent, but when he finally reached the waiting room outside the surgery where Gemma was being treated, admission was categorically refused. To make matters worse, the orderly in charge made it clear that this was at the patient's request.

'Nonsense,' Zen retorted. 'She doesn't even know I'm here.'

'The patient stated upon admission that if someone named Aurelio Zen asked to see her, permission should be refused.'

'But that's absurd! We live together!'

'The policy of the hospital is to respect the patient's wishes in such matters.'

The orderly turned away and began looking through a pile of files.

'How long will it be before the preliminary diagnosis is complete?' Zen demanded.

'That depends on the physician.'

'I'm asking for an estimate.'

'At least half an hour.'

Zen sighed loudly and wandered to the doorway shaking his head, nearly colliding with a tiny, wizened woman whose worn-out coat was at least five sizes too large for a physique heavily discounted by age.

'Bastards, they think they own you,' Zen muttered.

The woman tittered, an unexpectedly liquid ripple of sound. Zen suddenly recognised her as the person who had been talking to an apparently stuffed Pekinese in the bar near the football stadium the night before.

'Eh, no, it's the undertaker who owns you!' she replied.

Zen noted the time and went outside to have a cigarette, the ban on smoking inside the hospital apparently being observed in Bologna even by the doctors.

An ambulance had drawn up to the ramp outside the *Pronto Soccorso* department, and staff and paramedics were unloading a stretcher case under the supervision of two officers of the Carabinieri. In the tradition of policemen the world over, they had parked their car where it was most convenient for them and least so for everyone else, in this case blocking the wheeled route into the hospital. One of the officers went to move it, and on his way back Zen waylaid him and, having displayed his warrant card, enquired with mild professional curiosity what was going on.

'Gunshot wound,' the Carabiniere replied as the victim was conveyed inside.

Zen eyed the familiar bulging plastic bag that one of the paramedics held high, filled with colourless fluid feeding the intravenous drip, formerly his sole sustenance for days on end.

'Self-inflicted?'

'We don't know yet. He was in no condition to answer questions.'

'All part of the job,' Zen commented in a tone of trade solidarity.

'It's going to be news, though,' the other officer went on, seemingly piqued by the implication that this was just another routine chore.

'How so?'

'We checked his documents in the ambulance. Professor Edgardo Ugo. A big noise at the university, apparently.'

Zen frowned. The name sounded familiar, but he couldn't place it there and then. So much had happened in the past few hours.

'Well, I'd better go and see about taking a statement,' the patrolman remarked, straightening his cap.

'I'll tag along,' said Zen. 'I've got someone in there too.'

He was hopeful that Gemma might be undergoing treatment in one of the curtained-off areas of the emergency ward, and that by circumventing the orderly at the desk he might be able to talk to her. There must have been some mistake or confusion when she was checked in. She had very likely been mildly concussed. In any case, she would never refuse him in person.

Unfortunately the efficiency of the Bologna hospital and its deplorably adequate manning levels brought this scheme to nothing. Zen was intercepted and asked his business by a nurse, and once his identity and intent had been established he was referred to the ward sister, who ordered him to leave in no uncertain terms. As she escorted him to the door, they passed the cubicle where the Carabinieri patrolman stood watching the most recent admission being given an injection prior to the doctors cutting his clothing away. Zen smiled nostalgically. He had come to love those gleaming pricks of pain, as bright and shiny as the freshly unwrapped hypodermic itself, particularly when morphine was involved.

'That's him! That's him!'

The patient had raised himself up and was gesticulating wildly. Everyone turned to look, but by this time Zen and his wardress were out of sight behind the curtained side-screens, and a moment later the patient had slipped into unconsciousness.

. . . original contract specifically stipulated that payment would be made on receipt and acceptance – I emphasise the latter term – of a written report detailing your means, methods and findings in full.'

'I've told you what you wanted to know.'

'The presumption that you know what I "want to know" is impertinent.'

'But . . .'

'These photographs, for example,' Avvocato Amadori continued. 'I need to know where and when they were taken, with affidavits from credible witnesses in support of the foregoing facts.'

'Well, it was in this bar . . .'

'Has the proprietor of the establishment assented in writing to the photographic recording and subsequent reproduction and distribution of images of clients taken on his premises?'

'What?'

'I take it that means no.'

'Well . . .'

'So the said images are legally worthless.'

At the beginning of his solo career, Tony had considered making his slogan 'The hope of knowing everything, always', playing catchily on his surname. Plus he could have offered two plans at different rates, the Hope scheme and the Assurance scheme. 'Let me put it like this, Signora Tizia. "Assurance" is going to cost you a little more up-front, but think of it as an investment. It'll be well worth the extra in the long run, particularly if you ever decide to take the cheating son of a bitch to court.' In the end, though, he had rejected the

159

Hope option as too tentative. Now it seemed a massive presumption.

'You told me you wanted pictures of your son's low-life pals, *avvocato*. I've provided them, together with details of his address and movements over the last few days.'

'All you have provided me with is an assortment of photographs of various unappealing young men apparently in a state of advanced inebriation. Without objective evidence of their alleged connection with Vincenzo, over and above your verbal say-so, they are of merely anecdotal interest.'

With a father like this, no wonder the kid left home, thought Tony.

'And then there's the matter of your alleged expenses. You not only claim to have spent over three hundred euros on "refreshments and incidentals", but have the cheek to add a further five hundred and eighty to cover "depreciation of professional inventory"!'

'In the course of my investigations, I was mugged and robbed of a very valuable digital camera, which I had to replace in order to take those photographs, and of an equally expensive pistol.'

'I decline to be held responsible for losses due to your incompetence.'

'If you think I'm incompetent, *avvocato*, then why did you hire me?'

'To keep my wife quiet. The whole thing was her idea. Personally I'd be more than happy to let our ungrateful son discover the error of his ways in the fullness of time and at his own expense, but to maintain a semblance of peace in the household I judged it best to make a token gesture of concern. Not to the tune of almost fifteen hundred euros, however. On receipt and my acceptance of the full written report to which I have already alluded, I shall send you a cheque for the amount we originally agreed, together with a nominal five per cent per diem to cover your incidental outgoings.'

The line went dead. So, for a moment, did Tony. Then he reached for the bottle of Jack Daniels on his desk.

The offices of *Speranza Investigazioni SpA* occupied a small room at the back of a building whose legal status was currently indeterminate pending the outcome of a divorce case based largely on evidence gathered by Tony himself, who had foregone a percentage of his fee in return for the temporary use of this facility to house the 'janitorial security service' that he was supposedly providing, all on the strict understanding that when instructed to vacate the premises he would already have left, and indeed never have been there in the first place. Meanwhile Tony figured it was worth every cent, as he had been delighted to discover that the new European small change was called. It gave him a public face, a city centre letterhead, a window on the world and the opportunity to do all the things he would be doing at home in his suburban apartment anyway, only downtown.

It also gave him a base for his online operations, thanks to a tap into the DSL circuit installed in an apartment on the second floor. 'If I ain't heard of it, it never happened', Tony liked to say. Taken literally, this maxim would have erased almost all human knowledge from the record, but in practice it meant little more than a free subscription to a 'Headline HeadsUp' service that bombarded its clientele with news snippets in return for selling their email addresses to spammers offering cut-price, over-the-virtual-counter Viagra.

Feeling utterly defeated by his client's surly arrogance, Tony fired up the computer, logged on to his surveillance website and quickly tracked Vincenzo Amadori's movements that day, just in case the matter came up in future negotiations. They were fairly predictable: at home until eleven, half an hour in a café, and then the walk to the university that Tony had witnessed in person. An hour there, then back by a different route through the narrow streets of the former ghetto to the apartment he shared with Rodolfo Mattioli, the boyfriend of that cute illegal redhead.

'BREAKING NEWS' flashed the screen below a picture of a man graced with the aura of the modern celebrity: making you feel vaguely uneasy for not immediately recognising who he was. 'World-famed academic and author Edgardo Ugo shot in Bologna. The attack occurred outside the professor's house on Via dell'Inferno, in the heart of the city, shortly after one o'clock this afternoon. The victim was rushed to hospital but no details of his condition have yet been released. Earlier today, Professor Ugo was involved in a cookery contest against Romano Rinaldi, the star of the show *Lo Chef Che Canta e Incanta*, in an attempt to settle the issue of possible defamation resulting from Ugo's comments in his column for the weekly magazine *Il Prospetto*. The Carabinieri have stated that they are anxious to trace Signor Rinaldi's present whereabouts with a view to eliminating him from their ongoing enquiries.'

Tony felt a thought stir sluggishly in its comatose stupor. He couldn't care less if some professor had got shot by that celebrity chef, of course. No money in it for him. Nevertheless, something in that news bulletin had caught his attention. Via dell'Inferno – the Street of Hell, in the mediaeval ghetto – shortly after one o'clock that afternoon . . . He shot back to the online surveillance site, and carefully checked times and locations once again. Well now, he thought. Well, well. Well, well, well!

Ten minutes later he was in Amadori's law office. The receptionist put on a brave show of pretending that she hadn't been daydreaming about Tony ever since his previous visit, and then announced in a transparently insincere voice that *l'avvocato* was 'away from his desk'.

'I don't care if he's under it, honey,' Tony replied. 'Get him. But soon.'

By now visibly weak at the knees with barely repressed desire, the receptionist managed to blurt out that her employer could not be disturbed and suggested that Tony might care to make an appointment for the following month.

Tony Speranza eyed her appreciatively. The right age, he thought. Not that gleamy, raw look of uncooked sausages the flesh of the young ones had. This babe had been hanging just long enough. The meat was nicely cured without the casing getting too wrinkly.

'How much they paying you?' he said.

'*Mi scusi?*'

'Never mind. But if you want to make some extra, breathe the name Edgardo Ugo into your boss's shell-like ear.'

'Edgardo Ugo?'

Tony nodded.

'The great, and for all we know late, Professor Ugo.'

'What might this be regarding?'

'You going to go conditional on me, the possibilities are endless. Let's just say that Vincenzo Amadori, a young hooligan not entirely unrelated to your employer, was present in Via dell'Inferno at the time when Professor Ugo was shot, and that I can prove it with documented evidence that will stand up in any court of law. You got that, Wanda?'

The receptionist, damn her, blushed.

'How did you know my name?'

Mindful of the desirability of preserving his professional mystique, Tony forebore to point out the framed photograph that stood on the filing cabinet, with 'To Wanda, with all my love, Nando' scrawled across it. Some muscle-bound meatball with a chicken perched on his shoulder.

'Hey, once in a while you get lucky! And we just did,

Wanda. Because what I just told you is true, but so far you and I are the only people who know. I imagine that l'avvocato will want to keep matters that way, which gives us a certain leverage. Are you following me? So you go and drag him back to that old desk, by main force if necessary, and impress on him that if either of us were to make the Carabinieri a party to our exclusive knowledge, then those gentlemen would no doubt issue a pressing invitation for Vincenzino to assist them with their enquiries.'

He smiled and walked to the door.

'You make your deal, I'll make mine.'

'My husband's a policeman,' Wanda replied provocatively. Tony just laughed.

'Great! Let me know next time he's working nights, and we'll have dinner and compare notes.'

He was back in the bar he had patronised that morning, lingering over a quadruple Maker's Mark, when Amadori phoned. The conversation did not go entirely as Tony had foreseen. Not only did l'avvocato flatly refuse to offer any money in return for Tony's silence, still less to negotiate an appropriate sum, but proceeded to dismiss his hireling on the spot and with immediate effect, and threatened to have Speranza's private investigator's licence revoked for attempted extortion.

Tony switched to Jack Daniels for his second shot, feeling a need for its asperity to help him work out how to respond. This took less than five minutes. He then tossed back the bourbon and marched down the street to the junction with Via Rizzoli, where one of those museum pieces from an unimaginably primitive past, a public telephone box, had been retained as a heritage item. Tony stepped in and dialled Carabinieri headquarters. The response was a recorded woman's voice.

'Welcome to the Carabinieri helpline for the province of Bologna. If you know the extension number of the person you are calling, you may dial it at any time. To report a crime, please press 1. Alternatively, hang up now and dial 112 to reach our *pronto intervento* section. For information on our products and services, please press 2. To learn about career opportunities with the force, please press 3. To speak to a representative, please press 4 or hold the line.'

Tony Speranza did so, and was rewarded with an endless silence punctated at intervals by a different voice telling him that his call was important to them but that all operators were currently busy and the approximate wait time would be nine minutes. He slammed the phone down and called the Polizia di Stato. A surly male voice answered almost immediately. Tony wrapped the lapel of his greatcoat over his mouth and spoke rapidly in a generalised approximation of the local dialect.

'Listen, I know who shot that professor this afternoon. Name's Vincenzo Amadori, the lawyer's son. Can't give mine, but he's your man all right. I've got proof of that.'

He left the booth and walked quickly away. The police might trace the call eventually, but thanks to his gloves there would be no prints. Once the judicial machinery ground into motion then *il grande avvocato Amadori* might well decide that it had been rash of him to dismiss Tony's original offer. In fact, when the time came he might well raise the starting price, just to teach the smug bastard that you didn't fuck with Tony Speranza.

The original thirty minutes within which Zen had been told that he could expect to hear word of Gemma's condition stretched to an hour and more, divided between a series of coffees in a bar opposite the hospital complex and smoke breaks outside one or another of the doors, where a louring dusk was already well advanced. And when he finally lost patience on his fifth return to the desk, where a different orderly had now come on duty, and demanded to see Gemma at once, he was informed that she was no longer there.

'What do you mean?'

'She discharged herself.'

'Where did she go?'

The orderly shrugged.

'I have no idea.'

'Then let me speak to someone who does.'

'And who are you, *signore*?'

Zen decided that this was not the moment for worrying about the niceties of his civil status.

'Her husband.'

'*Un momento.*'

It was actually about twenty minutes before Zen was directed to an office on the second floor of the building where he was greeted by a tired-looking young man in a white coat.

'Signor Santini?' he said.

Zen nodded.

'Your wife left the hospital twenty minutes ago.'

'And you permitted this?'

The doctor shrugged.

'We have no power to detain patients. There were certain

additional tests I would have preferred to perform, but she refused them.'

'Where was she going?'

'I have no idea. Home, presumably.'

'Home?'

The doctor looked at him curiously.

'Back to Lucca, *signore*. Where she lives.'

'Was she in a fit state to drive?'

'I couldn't offer a qualified opinion on that question.'

Zen jerked his head angrily.

'If it had been your wife, would you have let her take the wheel?'

'No.'

Zen turned away feeling utterly cut adrift. He called Gemma's mobile. No reply. He was walking down the stairs to the foyer when, with a lift of his heart, he heard the muffled chirps of his own phone. But it turned out to be Bruno Nanni.

'*Buona sera, capo.* I'm so sorry to hear about your wife's accident. Those damn bikes can be as dangerous as a car. I had a near miss myself just the other day. I hope she's all right.'

'Oh yes, just minor scrapes and bruises. In fact she's already gone home.'

'Ah, right. So are you free this evening, by any chance?'

'Why?'

'Some interesting information has just come in. I don't want to discuss it on the phone, but it might potentially be an important lead and I think you should know about it as soon as possible. Is there any chance we might meet a bit later on?'

'Why not? God knows I've got nothing better to do.'

'There's a place in the university district called La Carozza. Five minutes walk from your hotel. Nothing fancy, just good pizzas and simple dishes, but we can talk freely there.'

'Sounds good.'

'Around nine?'

'I'll be there.'

But it soon began to look as though he wouldn't. As he crossed the hospital foyer, heading for the taxi rank, he was approached by a young man wearing the plainest of plain clothes who identified himself as an officer of the Carabinieri.

'You are Vice-Questore Aurelio Zen.'

It was not a question, so Zen did not reply.

'I have been ordered to place you under provisional arrest and take you to regional headquarters for questioning.'

Zen was so astonished that he could only murmur, 'On what charge?'

'Suspicion of attempted murder.'

A rancid darkness had fallen by the time Romano Rinaldi set out in search of sustenance for his soul. The cold that had gripped the city all week seemed if anything to have intensified, so it was perfectly natural that he should be wearing a scarf drawn up over his nose to ward off dangerous germs and potential lung infections, and coincidentally concealing his famous face. He had been worried about slipping out of the hotel unobserved, but ironically enough all attention in the lobby had been focused on two reporters pretending to be police detectives who were trying to browbeat the assistant manager into giving them a pass key to Signor Rinaldi's suite, and he felt reasonably confident that none of the other pedestrians trudging about the streets with an air of aimless intent would recognise him. As for the locales he planned to cruise, they would be dimly lit and packed with students, addicts, artists, anarchists and suchlike demographic flotsam and jetsam that definitely didn't form part of the core viewership of *Lo Chef Che Canta e Incanta*. Then, once he had restored his spirits, he would be off to that villa in Umbria, never to return to this accursed town.

He made his way slowly through the narrow streets of the university district, inspecting various locations with care. He was tempted for a moment by a pizzeria-cum-snack bar called La Carrozza, which had a handwritten sign in the window reading 'Temporary Kitchen Help Urgently Wanted', and appeared to be patronised by exactly the sort of people he was in search of. But service was at tables only, and once seated it would be difficult to make the kind of approach he had in mind. Besides, he would have to remove his scarf to eat or drink anything. Too risky, he decided.

One or two bars also looked likely propositions, particularly one darkened and smoke-filled dive where youths of various sexes wearing ethnic-looking knitted hats with earflaps perched on bar stools listening to American popular music beneath posters acclaiming *Il popolo di Seattle* and denouncing the World Trade Organization. But the place had almost the atmosphere of a private members' club, and Rinaldi would be the oldest person in the room and far too conspicuous.

In the end he found what he wanted on Via Zamboni, the main street of the quarter. It was one of the 'Irish pubs' that were now proliferating all over Italy. Cluricaune, as this one was called, was very spacious, on two levels, and packed with likely targets. Rinaldi fought his way to the bar and ordered a vodka martini. Although the place was stuffed with posters and statuettes of leprechauns, the use of the Irish language was limited to the name. Details of the cocktails and beers on offer, and of the establishment's 'Happy Hour', which was now in force, were all in English.

Drink in hand, Rinaldi nudged through the assembled throng, looking about him carefully. After a few moments he spotted a young man propped up on his elbows at the far end of the bar, an empty glass before him and his head lowered. He was wearing a black leather jacket with some sort of crest on the back, and looked drunk and very depressed. Rinaldi made his way through the crowd and stood to the man's left, close enough to attract his attention but not so close as to give offence. He lowered his scarf, which was beginning to suffocate him, downed his drink in one and signalled the barmaid.

'A large vodka martini,' he told her. 'And bring my friend here one too.'

The young man glanced at him sideways for a moment without straightening up.

'*Sono rovinato,*' he said tonelessly.

'Ruined?' Rinaldi echoed. 'Well, maybe I can help.'

He waited until the barmaid had come and gone before flashing some high-denomination banknotes at the other man.

'Good quality *coca*,' he said. 'The best on the market, the more the merrier, and immediately. If you can't deliver, there's a hundred in it for you to introduce me to someone who can.'

At first the youth did not react. I've picked the wrong man, thought Rinaldi, adjusting his scarf and preparing to move away. Then his companion straightened up with a weary sigh, downed his drink and laughed harshly.

'Sure, I can do that! Who cares now anyway? Let me make a few calls.'

He stepped back from the bar and immediately lurched sideways, completely off balance, clutching at Rinaldi with both arms for support. They clung together like two lovers for fully half a minute, before the younger man managed to stand upright on his own two feet, albeit swaying alarmingly.

'I'll be right back,' he announced defiantly.

Rinaldi had his doubts about that, but the youth hadn't asked for any money up front, so at worst the approach would have cost him a little time and the price of a drink. He cradled his glistening cocktail glass and gazed up idly at the TV mounted on brackets above the bar. Some game show was on, while a crawl bar at the bottom unscrolled the latest news headlines. Rinaldi watched idly, slurping his drink, as gnomic references to atrocities in the Middle East, domestic political feuding and the transfer of some football star danced across the screen. Then he almost dropped his glass. He thought he had seen his own name. But that item had already exited stage left, and he had to wait for the whole chorus line to go through their act again before it reappeared.

When it finally did, he wrapped the scarf around his face and made his way as quickly as the crush allowed to the door.

'Famous author Professor Edgardo Ugo shot in Bologna after cookery duel with star of *Lo Chef Che Canta e Incanta*. Police confident of imminent arrest'. This can't be happening, thought Rinaldi, striding head down along the tunnel of the long arcade. The wall and pillars were covered in hand-written 'Wanted' ads that now suggested something very different than the innocent pursuit of accommodation or employment. And maybe those two men who had been trying to get to him back at the hotel hadn't been reporters after all.

Still, it would surely be easy enough to establish his innocence. He had driven straight from the exhibition centre to his hotel and remained there all afternoon. Not only hadn't he shot Ugo, he couldn't possibly have done so. There was nothing to worry about.

A moment later, he realised that there was no way of proving that he had remained in his room all that time. He had locked the door, turned off the phone, instructed the management to refuse all visitors and had not been seen or heard by anyone until he finally summoned Delia to bring him the vodka, which might very well look as though he had belatedly been trying to establish an alibi. From the cops' point of view, of course, his public humiliation that morning would constitute one hell of a motive. Did anyone else have such good cause to shoot Ugo on this particular day? If not, he was inevitably going to be the prime suspect. And whatever ultimately came of it, his arrest at this crucial moment really would mean the end of everything. Not even Delia could spin him out of a murder charge.

'Well, *Aurelino mio*, here's another nice mess you've got us into.'

The speaker was a Carabinieri major in full uniform whom Zen recognised with subdued surprise as Guido Guarnaccia, a fellow Venetian who had served with the Carabinieri in Milan when Zen had been posted there many years previously. They had had professional dealings at the time, and even developed a sort of friendship, but when Zen had been transferred – to Bologna, ironically enough – they had lost touch.

Guarnaccia waved the detainee into a chair and dismissed his escort. He himself remained standing behind his desk.

'So, how are the children?' he asked after a stiffish silence.

'I don't have any children.'

'Ah. Right.'

'Although I may be about to become a grandfather.'

Guarnaccia stared at him.

'By proxy,' Zen explained.

'Ah, by proxy. By proxy. Right, right.'

Another silence supervened.

'And yours?' asked Zen.

Guarnaccia ignored this.

'You've put me in rather an awkward position, Aurelio.'

'Really?'

'Yes. Very awkward indeed.'

'I'm sorry.'

'Yes, well, it's all very well being sorry . . .'

Guarnaccia broke off.

'Luisetta got married last year,' he said.

'Congratulations,' Zen replied, wondering who the hell Luisetta was.

'To a photojournalist from Madrid.'

'Ah.'

'They'll speak Spanish.'

'At home?'

'The kids, I mean.'

Guarnaccia sighed deeply.

'I suppose you're aware that Professor Edgardo Ugo was shot this afternoon.'

'So I've heard.'

'The bullet struck some sort of sculpture outside his house and ricocheted into the poor man's left buttock. He's seriously injured and in considerable pain.'

'What's that got to do with me?'

'The victim alleges that he was involved in an accident in the adjacent street shortly before the shooting took place. He was cycling home after giving a lecture at the university when a woman came running out of a restaurant and collided with him. They both ended up on the ground. He further claims that a man then emerged from the restaurant, identified himself as one Aurelio Zen of the Polizia di Stato, and threatened to place Ugo under arrest for dangerous driving. Is this true?'

Zen limited himself to a confirmatory nod.

'Ugo says that you then called an ambulance. When it arrived, you told him that you couldn't proceed with an arrest since you had to accompany your lady friend to the hospital, but threatened to "take further steps" should she turn out to be seriously injured. According to his statement, however, you did not enter the ambulance when it left, but followed Ugo towards his house, where the shooting took place a few minutes later. His back was turned, so he was unable to identify his attacker, but the implication is obvious.'

Zen laughed lightly.

'Guido, I'm a Vice-Questore on special duties with the

Ministry in Rome. I don't run around waving pistols.'

Guarnaccia produced the same Delphic smile.

'Yes, I'd heard that you've risen quite high.'

'You too.'

'No fault of mine, I just outlasted the competition. Anyway, to clarify this point, you deny being armed at the time that this incident took place?'

'I haven't carried a gun for years, and if for some reason I needed one I would draw it from Supplies at the Ministry, where it would be duly logged out in my name. One phone call will prove that I have not done so.'

'Where were you on the evening that Lorenzo Curti was shot?'

Zen recalled that his former acquaintance, despite his lackadaisical manner, had not been without a certain glutinous intelligence.

'Tuesday evening?' he replied. 'Coming back from Rome. Why?'

'Because it looks as though the bullet that hit Ugo was fired from the same weapon that killed Curti. Unfortunately the bullet was too damaged by the impact with the sculpture to yield much forensic data, but the ejected cartridge case is a perfect match.'

Zen laughed again, as though trying gamely to enter into the spirit of his host's bizarre and slightly distasteful sense of humour.

'Well, in that case I'm in the clear! I was on the train between Rome and Florence at the time that Curti was murdered.'

'Can you present any witnesses to that effect?'

'Witnesses? Of course not. I mean, there were other people on the train. Not many, though. I bought a ham roll or something in the buffet car. The attendant there might remember me, although I doubt it. Little brunette. Uniform didn't suit her, or rather she didn't suit the uniform, which was designed by some misogynous fag in Trastevere who's decided that tits aren't being worn this year. I didn't get her name, but . . .'

'There are three problems from my point of view,' Guarnaccia broke in. 'First, pending a definitive forensic examination, the indications are that the weapon used in the Curti murder and the Ugo attack was almost certainly identical. Second, Ugo's statement, which is coherent and damning and has been confirmed by you, provides at least the semblance of a motive.'

He paused to light a cigarette, and possibly for effect.

'And the third problem?' asked Zen, digging out his battered pack of Nazionali.

'Ah!'

Guarnaccia's lips curled enigmatically once more. He really loved that smile, thought Zen. Perhaps he practised it in the bathroom mirror every morning after showering.

'The third problem is that you're a policeman.'

Zen savoured his cigarette for a luxurious moment, then laughed lightly.

'Isn't this taking inter-service rivalry a bit too far, Guido?'

'It's no joking matter,' Guarnaccia retorted with a touch of asperity. 'My reference is to the spate of serial killings that occurred in and around Bologna between 1987 and 1994, the so-called Uno Bianca slayings. Twenty-four victims in all, of whom six were members of this force. They were apparently selected opportunistically and gunned down by a gang of men driving a white Fiat Uno. The conspiracy theorists naturally believed that it was another *segreto di stato* like the bombing of the waiting room at the station, a right-wing plot to destabilise the political situation and punish "red" Bologna. Others, including myself, thought and continue to think that it was just a bunch of homicidal maniacs out on a thrill spree. But

whatever the truth about that, when the gang was finally cap-
tured it turned out to include five members of your force. In
fact the leader, Roberto Savi, was assistant chief of police at the
Questura here in Bologna at the time. It's thus hardly surpris-
ing that the Procura has directed us to undertake this investi
gation, and that I had no option, on the basis of the points I
have mentioned, but to have you brought in for questioning.'

Zen made a conciliatory gesture.

'I understand that, Guido, and I'll do everything I can to co-
operate. In fact, we can do better. I was sent up here by the
Viminale specifically to report back on the Curti investigation.
That will suit the Procura's conspiracy theory perfectly.'

'Why didn't you accompany your friend Signora Santini in
the ambulance as you had allegedly told Ugo that you would?'

'The paramedics said there was no space and told me to take
a taxi. You don't argue with doctors.'

This had the ring of truth, but was in fact the first lie that
Zen had told Guarnaccia. It had been Gemma herself who had
insisted that Zen should not accompany her in the ambulance.
'He's not my husband!' she'd kept shouting, much to everyone's embarrassment. 'I told him that and he yelled at me to
get out! That's why all this happened! Don't let him near me!'

'Ugo claims that you followed him.'

'I may have taken the same direction. I wasn't paying any
attention to him. It was simply the quickest way to the taxi
stand just off Piazza Maggiore. I wanted to be with my wife,
that's all.'

'According to the reports I have received, Signora Santini
denied – with some heat, I believe – that she is your wife.'

'Well, she isn't, strictly speaking, but . . .'

There was an embarrassed silence while they both waited to
see if Guarnaccia was going to pursue this point, but in the
end he chose another tack.

177

'How long did it take you to get a taxi?'

'I don't know. Ten minutes, perhaps.'

'So yet again you have no alibi for the time of the shooting.'

Zen shrugged impatiently to indicate that this joke was in poor taste and had gone on quite long enough. The resulting silence was broken by the ringing of the phone. Guarnaccia picked it up and listened in silence for some time. Then he turned to Zen with his patented smile.

'Well, Aurelino, you're in luck. That was Brunetti at the Questura. It seems that they've had an anonymous phone call identifying the man who shot Ugo. The informant also claims to have proof.'

'What sort of proof?'

'He didn't say.'

'So where does that get us?'

'It tips the balance ever so slightly. I personally never suspected for a moment that you were culpable, of course, but following Ugo's allegation I couldn't have been seen to take no action. Under these new circumstances, however, I feel that I can exercise my discretionary authority to release you, on condition that you undertake not to leave Bologna for the moment. Agreed?'

Zen thought of the cold bed that awaited him in Lucca.

'I'll be only too happy to remain here as long as you wish,' he replied.

Rodolfo Mattioli sat on an obdurate chair in a waiting room on the third floor of the hospital, a pile of magazines much thumbed by other hands on the table beside him. He was wearing a suit, his best shirt and tie, and had polished his shoes.

That afternoon, he had walked the streets and ridden the buses at random for hours before ending up in Cluricaune, where he had been approached by some bearded wrinkly who wanted to score cocaine. Normally Rodolfo wouldn't have got involved in anything like that, particularly with a stranger who might well be a nark, but after what he had already done, nothing seemed to matter any more. He'd feigned a near collapse at the bar and then, while apparently clutching him for support, had not only got rid of the incriminating pistol into his prospective client's overcoat pocket but also lifted the man's bulging wallet. After that he left the bar and ran back to the apartment he shared with Vincenzo.

There was no sign of the latter. Rodolfo peeled off the leather jacket he'd borrowed and flung it on to the pile of assorted clothing scattered on the floor of Vincenzo's bedroom, then quickly showered and changed into his most respectable outfit. He knew now, and with overwhelming certainty, what he needed to do, but there was no time to waste. He had been just about to leave when his mobile rang.

'I'm in deep shit, Rodolfo,' a dull, self-pitying voice declared. 'My dumb parents just called. Apparently the silly bastards hired a private investigator to find out where I was living and what I was doing. Now he's trying to blackmail them by claiming he has proof that I committed some crime.'

'What crime?'

'It's all bullshit, of course, but with a record like mine the cops will be after me in a Milan moment if he spills what he has to them. So I'm going to have to hide out for a while.'

'This all sounds a bit weird, Vincenzo. Are you fucked up?'

'No! This is real, God damn it! And what really pisses me off is that it's all my lousy parents' fault. Anyway, like I said, I'm going to have to go into deep cover for a while, only there's some stuff I need and I can't risk going back to the apartment. Can you meet me tonight with a bag full of clothes and some spare shoes?'

'Where?'

'Doesn't matter.'

Rodolfo thought a moment.

'Do you know a place called La Carrozza? Opposite San Giacomo.'

'I can find it.'

'I'll be there after nine with your stuff.'

Typical Vincenzo, thought Rodolfo as he hung up. Despite his denials, he was almost certainly on a paranoid stoner. If the cops did come round to their apartment asking questions, those questions would concern not Vincenzo but himself.

But that wouldn't happen, because he was going to forestall them by making a full and frank confession to the victim in person before turning himself in to the police right after seeing Flavia that evening. On the phone she had sounded guarded, almost cool, understandably enough after the way he had treated her the night before, but had agreed to meet him at La Carrozza. It would be tough to say goodbye to her, almost as tough as the inevitable prison sentence he would have to serve, but there was no other way to put a definitive end to the madness that had swept over him in the past few days.

In retrospect, Rodolfo conceded that Flavia might have been right about Vincenzo being a bad influence. Certainly his own behaviour had been unrecognisable, first taking the pistol that he had found hidden behind the books in his room, then following Edgardo Ugo back from the university lecture hall to his house in the former ghetto. For a moment it had looked as though he would be foiled by bad luck, when Ugo was involved in an accident with some woman who had come running out of a restaurant and collided with his bike. In the end, though, everything had gone according to plan. Well, almost everything.

Outside his town dwelling, Edgardo Ugo had caused an art work to be (re-)recreated, the high concept behind which he recounted to anyone who would listen – which necessarily included all his graduate students – at every possible opportunity. The house to the left of his stood slightly proud of the general alignment in the street, leaving a dark corner just beside Ugo's front door where drunks and homeless people were wont to urinate. A man as influential as Ugo could certainly have persuaded the city authorities to bar it off with a metal grid, as was normally done in the case of such illegal facilities, but he had instead come up with a typically witty and post-post-cultural solution.

Marcel Duchamp's 1917 ready-made *Fountain*, consisting of a mass-produced glazed ceramic urinal rotated on its horizontal axis, had long been an icon of the modernist movement. Ugo's stroke of genius had been to subject this signifier itself to a further stage of semiotic transformation (invoking the process of 'unlimited semiosis' and Lacan's 'sliding signified') by having it reproduced in the finest white Carrara marble and finished to the intense, glossy sheen associated with the sculptures of Antonio Canova – or, for that matter, mass-produced glazed ceramic ware. As with Duchamp's 'original', the finished piece had been mounted at ninety degrees to the vertical, in the filthy corner where derelicts went to pee furtively. But thanks to them this object functioned as a literal fountain,

181

the urine pouring out through the aperture for the mains inlet pipe on to the miscreant's trousers and shoes.

When Rodolfo had fired the pistol, while Ugo had his back turned to unlock his front door, this sculpture had been his intended target. The gesture was intended to be purely symbolic, a way of saying, 'Fuck you and your clever jokes and everything you stand for!' Instead, the bullet had deflected off the polished marble and must have ended up somewhere in Ugo's body. The victim had screamed and fallen over, while Rodolfo had taken to his heels. But now the time for running away was over.

A nurse came into the waiting area and approached him.

'Professor Ugo will see you now.'

Head bowed like a man on his way to the gallows, Rodolfo followed her down a long corridor. The nurse knocked lightly at one of the doors.

'Signor Mattioli is here.'

'*Va bene,*' said a familiar voice within.

The nurse withdrew.

'Ah, Rodolfo,' the voice said languidly. 'How very good of you to visit me. You of all people.'

The room was in almost total darkness. After the bright lights in the waiting area and corridor, Rodolfo could discern nothing.

'On the contrary, *professore*, it's very good of you to receive me,' he replied haltingly. 'I'm sorry to disturb you, only . . . Well, I've come in a hopeless but necessary attempt to apologise for . . .'

The answer was a soft laugh from the figure on the bed that Rodolfo could now just identify as such.

'That's all nonsense,' Ugo said.

Meaning, who cares about your apologies when I'm going to have you arrested the moment you leave, thought Rodolfo.

'Sit down, sit down!' Ugo went on. 'There's some sort of chair over there in the corner, I believe. I've been ordered by the powers that be to lie on my right side, so I can't turn to look at you, but we can still talk.'

Rodolfo found the chair and seated himself.

'Giacometti,' said the voice from the bed.

'Alberto?' queried Rodolfo, utterly at a loss.

'What do you know about him?'

Rodolfo scanned his memory.

'Italian Swiss, a sculptor and painter, born around 1900. Died some time in the 1960s, I think. Famous for his etiolated figures which express, according to some commentators, the pain of life.'

Ugo's laugh came again, louder and longer this time.

'*Bravo!* You were always my best student, Rodolfo, although of course I never told you that. Unless perhaps I did, by barring you from the class.'

'I want to apologise for that too. Absolutely and without any reservations. I think I must have gone slightly mad recently, but you see . . .'

He broke off.

'Yes?' queried Ugo.

Rodolfo hesitated a long time before replying.

'I think I'm in love, *professore*,' he heard himself say.

'Ah. In that case I won't detain you long. Anyway, what you may not know about Giacometti is that during his years in Paris he was run down by a bus while crossing the street. A friend he was with reported later that the artist's first words after the accident were, "Finally something has happened to me!" I've always thought it a good story, although I never really understood what Giacometti meant by that comment. But now I do, perhaps because something has finally happened to me.'

He fell into a silence which Rodolfo did not attempt to break.

'I've been thinking of writing a book,' Ugo said at last. 'For years, I mean. Cornell, early 1980s. Wonderful campus, magnificent library. Some reference text in English. I've never been able to remember which.'

'The *Anglo-American Cyclopedia*,' Rodolfo replied without thinking.

After a moment, Ugo laughed heartily, then moaned.

'Ow! Yes, yes, very good. Borges' Uqbar. But this wasn't the forty-sixth volume of anything. Much earlier in the alphabetical series of *voci*. It was entitled, in gold-blocked letters on the spine, "BACK to BOLOGNA", those being the headings of the first and last articles in that particular volume.'

'A completely random phrase.'

'Utterly. You may remember the fuss that Zingarelli ran into when the eleventh edition of their dictionary featured *masturbazione* as the headword in bold type on one page. Anyway, most of the volumes of the work I saw on the stacks at Cornell were entitled with quite meaningless phrases. "HOW to HUG", for example. Ridiculous.'

'I'm not so sure about that.'

Ugo's smile, if not visible, was audible.

'Well, you may of course be better informed than I. At all events, this experience made me realise two things. One was the obvious fact that I was homesick, my research project was stalled, and the only way that I could salvage something from it was by going back to Bologna.'

'Which you did?'

'I came home, yes. And, as it turned out, wrote the book that really launched my career. What I didn't write was the second thing suggested to me by that reference work in the library at Cornell, namely *Back to Boulogne*, a mystery in which the detective solves nothing. For my protagonist I had in mind a certain Inspecteur Nez, playing on the French word for nose, as in "has a nose for" but also "led by the nose". In short, at once a deconstruction of the realistic, plot-driven novel and an *hommage* to Georges Simenon, the master of Robbe-Grillet and hence in a sense of us all. Any amount of atmosphere and sense of place, in other words, but no solution, just a strong final curtain line.'

Rodolfo stole a glance at his watch.

'Why not scrap the sense of place too?' he murmured.

The patient was silent for a moment.

'Like a late Shakespearian romance, you mean?'

'Why not?'

'Located in a notional site named Illyria or Bohemia or . . .'

'Ruritania.'

'That's been done.'

'Surely the whole point is that everything's been done.'

Professor Ugo was silent for some time. When he spoke again, it was in a distinctly crisper tone.

'Possibly. At any rate, the reason I gave the nurse permission to admit you, Mattioli, was that I wanted to announce a decision that I've come to regarding what has happened.'

Rodolfo sighed. Here it comes, he thought.

'I just don't know what to say, *professore*. Apologies are obviously useless. No one could forgive what I've done to you.'

'That seems a little extreme,' Ugo replied. 'But even if I couldn't forgive, I can at least forget. In fact, I've already forgotten. So come back to the seminar, write your thesis and take your diploma. You're an intelligent if rather forthright young man with your life to lead, a life in which many things will happen to you. Perhaps one already has. I believe you said that you were in love.'

'I think I am.'

'The distinction is specious. And now I must ask you to go. I'm still quite weak, but the doctors say that I'll be back on my feet, if not my bum, by next week. So I expect to see you in class then. Understand?'

Rodolfo didn't understand in the slightest.

'*Grazie infinite, professore,*' he said, and left.

After his conditional release from the clutches of the Carabinieri, Zen felt like a drink. On the other hand, he didn't fancy returning to the bar near his hotel, where half the clientele, judging by the stacked trophies and plaques on display, were high-ranking officers from the Questura. He'd had enough of cops for one day.

In the end he stumbled on the perfect refuge in a side street off the market area. The customers here were drawn from a much broader social range than at Il Gran Bar, and were less interested in showing off their status and style than in chatting animatedly, drinking deep and pigging into the astonishing range of non-fat-free appetisers piled high on the bar: glistening cubes of creamy mortadella, chewy chunks of crisp pork crackling, jagged fragments of golden *stravecchio* Parmesan. The Lambrusco was of the increasingly scarce authentic variety, unfiltered and bottle-fermented. On that bleak evening, when the gelid smog in the streets seemed not just a meteorological fact but a malign presence, its rich purple froth provided a welcome confirmation that there was more to life than hospitals, police stations and faithless lovers.

Most people are familiar with the temporary euphoria produced by a few glasses of wine, but few would claim that the experience had saved their marriage. For Zen, however, this may just have been the case, because when his phone rang he was in a particularly mellow and affable mood, amenable to anything and treating it all lightly.

'It's me,' Gemma's voice said.

'At last! How are you? Where are you?'

'In a bar.'

'Me too.'

He laughed.

'We really must stop meeting like this.'

There was no reply, but instead of regretting his flippancy and moodily clamming up in turn, he signed the bartender to refill his glass and carried on as though there had just been a brief lapse in transmission, of no personal intent or significance.

'Which bar? I'll come immediately.'

'No, no, don't. Stefano's here.'

'Stefano?'

'My son.'

'Oh, Stefano! Yes. Yes, of course. I thought you said . . . er, "*sto telefono*".'

'You're the most awful liar, Aurelio.'

'That's because I never get any practice.'

'Anyway, the reason I'm calling is . . . I'm having dinner with them, as I told you. Then I was planning to drive home, but after what's happened I'm not so sure that would be a good idea.'

'Don't dream of it, particularly in the dark. The truckers on the autostrada are vicious. The doctor I spoke to at the hospital was horrified that you'd even discharged yourself. He said you needed more tests and . . .'

'It's not just that. But I really need a bed for the night, only because of this trade fair there don't seem to be any hotel rooms to be had.'

'Do you want to sleep with me?' Zen replied in a lighthearted tone that he had thought he would never be able to manage again.

'If that's what it takes.'

'It's a sort of bed and a half rather than a full double.'

'I'll take it.'

He laughed again, quite naturally.

'It's yours, *signora*. We'll just need a credit card number to secure the deposit. I had an appointment this evening, but I'll cancel it.'

'Don't do that. I won't be free till later anyway. Probably much later. They've had some bad news, you see. That's why Stefano arranged to meet me here before dinner, so that he could break it to me alone. Anyway, it looks like being a long evening in every sense.'

'What's happened?'

'I'll tell you later. But the upshot is that I'm not going to be a grandmother after all.'

This was a much stiffer check, but once again Zen carried blithely on.

'That's a shame. Still, they're young. There's plenty of time.'

'Not necessarily. It sounds as though this has put the relationship at risk. I get the feeling that Stefano's relieved, quite frankly. Lidia, on the other hand, is naturally shattered. So a long evening, and I may be a bit weepy when we meet. It's been a difficult day, one way and another.'

Zen took another hearty gulp of the effervescent wine and started toying with one of the pork *ciccioli*.

'Yes, shame about lunch. You misunderstood me. I was talking to my stomach.'

'I'd rather been looking forward to knitting little bootees and jackets.'

'Well, I could use a new pullover.'

'It wouldn't be the same.'

He laughed again, by now quite impervious to anything she might throw at him.

'I should hope not! It would never fit otherwise. I'll tell the hotel to expect you. Just ask at the desk and they'll give you a key if I'm not back.'

'Thank you.'

'All part of the service, *signora*. We know you have a choice. We work hard to be both your first choice and your last.'

He hung up, grinning widely, and grabbed a lump of Parmesan the size of an inoperable tumour.

'But this is crazy!' the barber protested. 'You have a magnificent head of hair, a superb beard! All that's required is a delicate and discreet trim, a snip here, a hint more shape there . . .'

'Do what I say!' snapped Romano Rinaldi.

For a moment the barber, reflected in the mirror facing the swivel chair in which Rinaldi was seated, looked as though he might be about to refuse. The man must have been in his sixties, with a moonlike face and the expression of a priest struggling to bring an unrepentant sinner to the foot of the cross, while his shop looked as though it had been furnished about the time of national unification and left untouched ever since. The proprietor clearly regarded himself as one of the city's top professionals, and was more accustomed to advising his clients on which interventions needed to be undertaken than merely carrying out their orders, particularly when these were eccentric and wilful in the extreme. Nevertheless, he picked up his scissors with a heavy sigh of disapproval and set to work.

His eyes fixed on the antique sink in front of him, Rinaldi sat there impassively as his shorn locks fell on to the wrap that covered his upper torso. The police would be watching the hotel, the railway and bus stations, and the airport, as well as monitoring both his and Delia's mobile phones. He had instructed the barber to shave his scalp bald, remove his eyebrows and trim his beard down to a very thin moustache. That should prevent any casual recognition on the street. His plan was to find a small, seedy hotel of the kind used by young backpackers on a tight budget, pass himself off as a foreigner and tell the proprietor that his passport had been stolen but he had informed the consulate and a replacement would arrive within the week. That and a hefty deposit should do the trick in the short term. After that it would be a matter of keeping an eye on the news and seeing how the affair played out.

The barber finished his job, scowling his disapproval, and whisked away the hair-covered wrap.

'Fifty euros.'

Getting to his feet, Rinaldi stared speechlessly at his reflection in the mirror while the barber brushed him down like a horse. Even Delia wouldn't recognise him like this, he thought. He reached for his wallet, but encountered only an alien object, smooth, cool and heavy. Pulling it out impatiently, he found to his amazement that he was holding what looked like an automatic pistol.

It took him only a moment to work out that the little rat at the Irish bar had ripped him off after all. He'd faked that collapse to give him the chance to grab hold of Rinaldi, then lifted his wallet and substituted this cheap replica gun to simulate its bulk and weight. A wave of sheer panic swept over him as the implications sunk in. All his cash and credit cards were gone, and since he was wanted by the police he could not report the incident and get replacements in the usual way.

He turned to the barber, flashing his radiant Lo Chef smile.

'Look, I seem to have left my wallet at home.'

The man did not reply. He stood very still, gazing down at the pistol in his client's hand. Rinaldi hastily replaced it.

'I'll leave my watch as surety while I go and fetch my wallet,' he went on. 'It's a vintage Rolex, platinum band, worth at least a thousand. I'll be back in about half an hour.'

'I close in ten minutes,' the barber stated in a voice like an automated recording.

'Then tomorrow.'

He thrust the watch at him and walked out. As soon as he reached the corner, he turned left and ran until he was out of breath. The night air felt cruelly cold in his newly shorn state, but at least there was no one about. A few metres further on, lost in the overarching shadows cast by the *portici*, stood a municipal rubbish bin. Rinaldi rooted about in it until he found an empty plastic bag, and then stuffed his pigskin gloves, cashmere scarf and camelhair overcoat into it. Then he roughed up his blazer, pullover and trousers against the rough plaster on one of the pillars of the arcade, scuffed his immaculately polished brogues repeatedly against a neighbouring doorstep, and set off again looking rather more like a common vagrant, battered bag of belongings in hand.

But where to? The loss of his wallet changed everything. He was not only homeless and wanted by the police, but down to four euros and sixty-three *centesimi* in small change, most of which he promptly spent in the first bar he came to, just to warm up. He was staring at the drying stain in his coffee cup, as though hoping to read his fortune in the grounds, when a memory of something he had seen earlier that evening came back to him. He cringed with humiliation at the very idea. What a comedown! Talk about riches to rags. But there was no obvious alternative, and it might just prove to be what he needed to see him through the next few days, until things sorted themselves out. It was certainly worth a try.

Flavia looked up from her battered paperback at the clock above the alcove where the proprietor was busily crafting raw pizzas beside the maw of the oven. One of the two waiters reappeared, the skinny Stan Laurel lookalike. He regarded her quizzically.

'Ready to order?' he asked, when Flavia did not react.

'I'm waiting for someone.'

And he was more than twenty minutes late, she thought, as the waiter sidled off. It had been absurdly naïve to imagine that he would come at all. Her relationship with Rodolfo had been intense, diverting and instructive, but she had never allowed herself any illusions about the ultimate outcome, even before he started acting in this strange, angry, icily controlled way. But with his university career in ruins, there was no longer any reason for him to remain in Bologna, or with her. That was what he had been hinting at last night, taunting her with lying about her origins and then refusing to sleep with her. As for this evening, he simply wouldn't show up, leaving her to get the message. But she already had.

She glanced up hopefully as the door opened, but it was a stranger, as tall and austere in appearance as her own dead father. Flavia finished the chapter she had been reading and then consulted the clock again. The thirty minutes grace she had allowed Rodolfo had passed. She put on her coat and headed for the door.

'I'm sorry,' she said to the fat waiter, who was serving two pasta dishes to a nearby table. 'My boyfriend just phoned to say he can't make it.'

Ollie inclined his head sideways in a way that could have meant anything or nothing.

In the street just outside, she literally ran into Rodolfo. He dropped the duffle bag he was carrying and kissed her on the mouth.

'Everything's all right!'

They returned together to the table that Flavia had vacated, the only one free now that half of the rest had been pushed together to form a large rectangular area seating about a dozen, presumably for a group that would arrive later. Rodolfo stowed the nylon bag in the corner and then, in a breathless rush, told Flavia that he had been to see Professor Ugo in hospital, had been readmitted to the course, and could finish his thesis and graduate.

'That's wonderful,' said Flavia coolly. 'Then what?'

Rodolfo shrugged.

'Come the summer, I'll want to go back to Puglia, at least for a while. My father says he needs me, although who knows how long that will last. Anyway, I'm sick of this damned place. Afterwards we'll see.'

Flavia nodded vaguely.

'What's the weather like in Puglia?'

'Ah, much warmer than here! The people too.'

She pointedly did not respond.

'And in Ruritania?' he asked with a self-deprecating smile.

'The weather in Ruritania? It doesn't exist.'

Rodolfo took her hand.

'I'm sorry, Flavia. I was so angry about what had happened, almost insane, and I took it out on you. I apologise.'

There was a silence.

'What's in the bag?' Flavia asked at length.

'Oh, just some clothes Vincenzo asked me to bring him. Apparently he's going to be away for a while and couldn't get back to the apartment. The reason that I was so late getting here is I had to go back and pick that up after visiting Ugo.'

He smiled at her.

'Anyway, enough about all that. Let's talk about us.'

'Us?'

'Will you come with me to Puglia?'

She gazed at him for at least a minute, levelly and without the slightest expression.

'As what?'

Rodolfo mimed exaggerated shock and horror, silent film style.

'As my *fidanzata*, of course! They'd stone us both to death otherwise.'

Stanlio manifested himself at the table.

'Two margheritas with buffalo mozzarella,' Rodolfo told him, not breaking eye contact with Flavia. 'And a bottle of champagne.'

'. . . a bottle of *spumante*,' the waiter repeated, writing on his pad.

'No, not *spumante*. French champagne.'

The waiter looked doubtful.

'I could get some from the bar down the street. But the price . . .'

Rodolfo produced a well-stuffed designer wallet, an evidently expensive item that Flavia didn't recall having seen before.

'Is irrelevant,' he said.

As a newcomer to La Carrozza, Aurelio Zen had been allocated a small table set apart between the end of the bar and the front door. This afforded a close-up view of interactions between the overworked waiters and the foulmouthed owner, with much interesting commentary on both sides, and a blast of freezing air whenever the door opened to offset the searing heat of the wood-burning pizza oven at Zen's back. He ordered a glass of beer but no food, on the grounds that he was waiting for someone.

'Eh, like everyone!' the thinner of the two waiters had replied cryptically.

Zen looked around the premises, but the only person who seemed to fit the waiter's comment was a young woman sitting at a table near by, who kept glancing up from her book at the front door. She had surveyed Zen for a moment when he entered, with a look of hopeful eagerness that immediately faded as recognition failed. She had blue eyes of the most astonishing clarity, as bright and guileless as ice, but much warmer. She was very attractive in other ways too, and Zen found his own gaze returning to her both for this reason and because the title of the book that she was reading seemed to be *The Prisoner of Zen*, although her plumply elegant forefinger partially covered it.

In the end she gathered up her things and left, rather to his disappointment, only to collide in the street outside with a young man who kissed her spectacularly and then led her back to her table, where the couple were now canoodling and chatting enthusiastically over a bottle of bubbly wine. 'Ah, youth!' thought Zen, glad to have someone to feel happy for.

Now that his brief interlude of high spirits – probably a delayed reaction to the shock of his arrest – had passed, his own prospects for the evening seemed considerably less promising. The news that Stefano's girlfriend had miscarried promised to add a vast new uncharted minefield to the blighted war-zone that his relationship with Gemma had become. He had apparently acquired an almost infinite capacity for saying or doing the wrong thing, and this new development, which could hardly fail to be the main topic of conversation between them in the immediate future, offered plenty of scope for his talents in this respect.

It was then that a thought occurred to him. As matters stood, he had no real standing in the Santini family, but as Stefano's stepfather he would have to be accorded at least a grudging toleration. So if the situation started to get out of hand back at the hotel later that evening, he would simply make a proposal of marriage to Gemma. That would at least clarify the situation, whatever the result. If she turned him down, they would have to part. If she accepted, they would have to put up with each other. It might not be the most romantic solution, but it was eminently practical.

Another ten minutes passed before Bruno Nanni finally turned up.

'So what's this "important lead" you mentioned?' Zen demanded once they had ordered their pizzas. 'You were very mysterious about it on the phone.'

Bruno leant forward.

'Well, apparently some anonymous informant called the Questura this afternoon . . .'

'Claiming he knows who shot Edgardo Ugo,' Zen interrupted. 'Stale news, Bruno. The Carabinieri told me hours ago.'

'You've been in touch with the Carabinieri?'

'They got in touch with me. The officer in charge of the Ugo shooting is an old friend of mine and a fellow Venetian. He naturally wanted to compare notes.'

'Did they tell you the name that the caller mentioned?'

Zen thought back.

'No, actually they didn't mention a name.'

Bruno smiled smugly.

'They couldn't, because we haven't told them.'

'How come you know all this, Bruno?'

'Got it out of the duty sarge who took the call.'

Their pizzas arrived, and for some time both men were absorbed in eating.

'Do you also know the name involved?' asked Zen when his first wave of hunger had passed.

Bruno was in the middle of chewing a gargantuan bite and couldn't reply immediately.

'Vincenzo Amadori,' he finally replied in a choked whisper.

'Probably just a nuisance call.'

Bruno shook his head.

'There's been no public reference to the ballistics tie-in between the two cases,' he pointed out. 'The buzz around the Questura is that the same gun was definitely involved, but they're not going to release that news to the media for fear of setting off an Uno Bianca feeding frenzy. It looks like they're going to keep it under wraps for a while, with the excuse that further tests are needed, and hope to get a quick break in the case before they have to come clean.'

He finished his beer and signalled the waiter to bring a refill.

'And without the knowledge that the same gun was used, there would be no point in anyone trying to smear Vincenzo with the Ugo affair. I doubt he even knew who Ugo was, never mind had a motive to shoot him.'

Zen felt a sudden sense of lassitude and indifference, a brief backwash from the storm that had so recently threatened to overwhelm him.

'Well, that's the basic problem with the whole investigation,' he heard himself say, as though at a great distance. 'On the face of it, the two victims had nothing whatever in common beyond the fact that they were well-known public figures in Bologna. There are plenty of killers who attack only certain demographic groups, usually prostitutes, but celebrity stalkers are invariably obsessed with one particular person. No others need apply.'

'Perhaps there were two men involved,' Bruno suggested, waving a forkload of pizza in the air. 'One shot Curti for reasons of his own, the other Ugo ditto, but with the same pistol.'

'You should retire and write thrillers,' said Zen sarcastically 'Anyway, it no longer has anything to do with us. On the basis of the possible analogy you mentioned, the judicial authorities have handed over the Ugo case to our colleagues in the Carabinieri. Assuming that the ballistics tests verify the identity of the weapon concerned, they will get de facto control of the Curti murder as well, leaving us free to deal with such really important issues as policing football games.'

He broke off as a party of about a dozen entered the establishment, laughing and chatting loudly, filed past Bruno and Zen and took their places at the large table that had been assembled at the back of the room. One of the waiters appeared and collected the empty pizza plates.

'*Tutto bene, signori?*'

Zen nodded, but Bruno scratched the back of his neck.

'You go if you want, *capo*, but I'm still hungry.'

A man in a filthy apron had just emerged from the rear of the premises to lay two plates of pasta on the counter next to the pizza oven. He was pudgy, with a bald head, a vestigial moustache, no eyebrows and an air of immense resentment.

'Who's that?' Bruno asked the waiter.

'The new help. Normo's mother's been taken poorly, so we had to get someone at short notice to do the made dishes.'

'Is he any good?'

'He's only just started. A foreigner. I haven't had any complaints. *La nonna* is keeping a close eye on him.'

'God help him. Well, let's see how good a team they make. Bring me a bowl of *penne all'arrabbiata* and half a litre of red.'

'In that case, I'll have a dessert,' said Zen. 'That chocolatey thing on the bottom shelf of the cooler.'

Behind them, the whoops, giggles and guffaws from the large table soon rose to such a level that there was no need for Bruno and Zen to try and find something to talk about.

'One *penne all'arrabbiata*,' the waiter shouted to the chef.

Shit, thought Romano Rinaldi, how the hell do I make that? But the vigilant crone perched on a tall stool in the corner was already on the job.

'Don't just stand there gawping! Get the pasta in! Two handfuls. Stir it well until it comes to the boil, the water's getting gluey and it might stick. Drain that pot, refill it and switch to the backup. Warm up a ladleful of tomato sauce, add a pinch of chilli and . . .'

For the second time that day, Romano Rinaldi set a huge pan of pasta boiling. This time, though, he made sure that it didn't boil over. This totally sucks, he thought. From being the celebrated and beloved *Chef Che Canta e Incanta* to being bullied and ordered around by some vicious granny who had once again got her hands on a man whose life she could make a misery, and was relishing every opportunity to do so.

And Romano gave her plenty. Not only did he not know how to cook, he deeply and indeed viscerally loathed the entire process. What he loved was celebrating the idea of tradition, of authentic shared experience and a stable and loving home life around the family hearth. Cooking was the medium he had chosen for this, but in itself it was a messy, painstaking, unrewarding and – as he had demonstrated so spectacularly that morning – potentially very dangerous form of drudgery that demanded total concentration and offered at best a sense of relative failure. Who has not always the impression of having eaten a better meal than the one set before them? It was a mug's game, which was no doubt one reason why it had traditionally been left to women.

These large philosophical questions apart, Romano Rinaldi had ample specific reasons for feeling utterly miserable. A splitting headache for one, the result of his earlier indulgences and current lack of either drugs or alcohol to satisfy his urgent medical needs. Then there was *la nonna*, of whom the less said the better, and the unutterably vile surroundings in which he was forced to go about his distasteful and humiliating chores.

The pizzas that were the mainstay of the establishment were prepared and baked by the owner and his son in a spotlessly clean extension of the bar, in full view of the clientele. The kitchen area at the rear of the premises where he was penned up, well out of sight, was substantially smaller than any of the walk-in cupboards in Rinaldi's Rome residence, and every surface was exuberantly filthy. The place looked like the scene of some Mafia settling of accounts after the bodies had been removed. Red splashes covered the pitted plaster walls, which were marked by long vertical gouges that might well have been made by the fingernails of some dying mobster. The floor was sprinkled with what at first looked like capers flung about with mad abandon, but turned out on closer inspection to be rat droppings. Rinaldi had been sorely tempted several times already to walk out and take his chances with the police. Even if he ended up getting convicted, could a prison term with hard labour be any worse than this?

When he had asked about the job a few hours earlier, the surly proprietor had at first shaken his head, then abruptly changed his mind and told the supposed illegal immigrant that he would give him a trial, starting immediately, but only because there was a large birthday party booked for that evening and he was desperate for someone, anyone, to help out in the kitchen. It had also been made clear to Rinaldi that he was to follow the orders of Normo's grandmother to the letter, she being ninety years old and unable to do the work herself. 'She's the brain, you're the robot,' was how the charmless owner had succinctly summed up the situation. 'And don't even fucking dream of showing your horrible face in the dining area. Just bring the dishes out when they're ready, set them down here on the counter and get straight back to work.'

The only upside of the whole situation was that his anonymity appeared to be complete. No one had given the slightest sign of realising who he was, or indeed of being aware of him at all except as an object for their use or in their way. He had become part of the immigrant stealth population, fully visible yet barely perceived, less real in his actual being than he had been as a two-dimensional image on television. Certainly no one would ever remark on the similarity between the two, or if they did would instantly dismiss the thought as a category error of the most basic kind. For the moment, anyway, he was safe.

But not from *la nonna*.

'Don't stand there scratching your arse! Drain the pasta, then empty and refill the pot, saving a splash of the cooking water to loosen the sauce.'

As usual, her orders were not in sequence, and he had to try and work out what to do first. Being a good cook was all about timing, he was beginning to realise, and his was terrible. Worse was to come. The pot of pasta water, as thick as soup after many uses, was hotter and heavier than Rinaldi realised, until a blossoming cloud of steam from the sinkward gush scalded his face and he dropped it on his foot.

'*Macché?*' the stooled crone howled, glaring at her cringing serf. 'Did your mother have to teach you to shit? Leave it, leave it! Dish the pasta, add the sauce and a sprig of parsley and take it out. Quick, quick, before it gets cold!'

Then, in a terrible screech: 'ANTOOOOOOONIO!!!'

It was a blessed relief to escape from the kitchen, even limping and for only a few seconds. Having set the plate down, Rinaldi stole a look at the group assembled for the birthday festivities, exactly the kind of extended family occasion that he had so often hymned on his show. To think that just that morning he, *Lo Chef Che Cuntu e Incunta*, would secretly have despised such people and their vulgar *piccolo-borghese* jollifications.

The waiter snatched the dish of pasta from the counter and handed Rinaldi a piece of paper.

'Nine orders for the large party. All to be ready together, so move it!'

It was a tribute to the vigorous if crude skills of Vincenzo Amadori's hair stylist that when he entered La Carrozza, neither Bruno nor Rodolfo recognised him at first. Vincenzo had spent much of the afternoon at a hair salon in an unfashionable suburb having his rug cut, dyed pink and spiked in retropunk mode. Spotting Rodolfo and his Ruritanian tart at their usual table, Vincenzo slouched over and plonked himself down.

'Got the bag?'

Rodolfo jerked a thumb at the corner behind his chair.

'Right then, I'll be off,' said Vincenzo, getting to his feet again.

'Oh, calm down!' Rodolfo replied. 'And sit down. No one's going to pick you up here looking like that. In either sense of the phrase. So stay and have a drink with us, at least. Flavia and I have something to celebrate.'

He signalled to the waiter to bring another glass. Vincenzo leered at the bottle.

'Veuve Clicquot? Sort of pricey shit my parents and their set drink to impress each other. What the fuck's this all about? You win the lottery or something?'

'In a way,' Rodolfo replied with a long look at Flavia. 'We just got engaged.'

Vincenzo slewed his head like a startled horse. The extra glass arrived, and Rodolfo did the honours.

'Here's to all of us!' he proposed gaily.

He and Flavia clinked glasses. Vincenzo downed his dose in one, scowled and lit a cigarette.

'You don't seem very happy for us,' Flavia remarked.

Vincenzo shrugged.

'For you, maybe. Not for me.'

'Why not?'

'Other people's happiness brings me bad luck.'

A soggy silence followed.

'So what exactly is all this about?' asked Rodolfo, jerking a finger at Vincenzo's hairdo and a thumb at the bag of clothing he had brought.

Vincenzo drew a small bottle of some clear spirit from his pocket and had a long slug.

'I told you, fuckwit!'

'You said that the private detective your parents hired to check up on you claims to have evidence that you committed a crime. What crime?'

Vincenzo squirmed uneasily in his chair.

'It doesn't matter.'

'Meaning you don't trust us.'

'It doesn't matter, that's all. Okay, it was the thing that happened today. That prof at the uni got plugged.'

'You didn't do that!' Rodolfo exclaimed.

'Of course I didn't! Even if the cops find me, they'll never be able to prove a thing. I just don't need the hassle, that's all. That's why I'm going to lie low for a while."

'Can't you prove that you were somewhere else at the time?'

'I was asleep.'

'Alone?'

'Listen, I didn't fucking do it, okay? This time I'm completely and utterly innocent.'

Rodolfo nodded seriously.

'I know you are,' he said. 'You see . . .'

'This time?' Flavia put in.

Vincenzo gave her a hard look, as though recognising her as an equal. He's never looked at me like that, Rodolfo thought.

'Well, I did Curti! I've been telling everyone that until I'm blue in the face, but of course the bastards don't believe me when it's the truth. Instead they try and nail me over this lie.'

'So you killed Lorenzo Curti,' Rodolfo remarked, just to remind them both that he was still there.

'Sure. I'd been carrying that Parmesan cutter around for weeks. My first idea was to carve up the paintwork on his car when he was at one of the games down here and leave the knife at the scene to make a statement.'

He laughed raucously.

'Get under his skin a bit, know what I mean? But I never had a chance. He always had one of his minders with him, or some business buddy.'

He jerked back another drink.

'But that night in Ancona everything came together. After the game I hung around the VIP entrance to the stadium, and for once Curti came out alone. He knew my father and he'd seen me around the house back when I used to live there. So when I told him that I'd missed the fan bus and asked for a lift back to Bologna he waved me into his Audi. He came off the autostrada at San Lázzaro to let me out, and when he pulled over I let him have it. Then I stuck the cheese cutter in his chest and walked home. Nice touch, don't you think? The Parmesan knife, I mean.'

'What did you talk about on the drive back?' Flavia enquired.

Vincenzo stared at her in utter bewilderment.

'What the fuck's that got to do with it?'

'Where did you get the gun?' Rodolfo demanded, in an intentionally ironic parody of the typical *commissario di polizia*, given to fixed ideas and the third degree. Vincenzo laughed uneasily and flashed one of his rare radiant smiles, switching effortlessly into his alternative persona as someone gifted with beauty to burn, who could not only get away with anything but make you long for him to try.

'I came by it,' he said, waving his hand as though to suggest that firearms regularly fell into it by some process that he did not understand but was powerless to prevent.

'Oh come on!'

'No, really. There was this old guy in the bar, right?'

'Where?'

'At Ancona, after the game. He was taking photographs of me and the boys with that camera I showed you and I sussed that he must be the snooper my parents had hired. They hadn't told me, natch, but the housemaid gave me a heads-up. So when the guy goes to pee I go in after him and smash his head against the wall, then go through his pockets. And I find the camera, very nice job too, full of digital shots of us, and also a pistol.'

Vincenzo frowned.

'And then someone took it! From our apartment. I'd hidden it behind the books in your bedroom.'

He shot Rodolfo a glance.

'It was you, wasn't it?'

'Of course not!'

'Then who?'

'The private detective, of course,' said Flavia. 'He must have been keeping a watch on the house, because he followed me back to mine and then came round later and tried to pump me for information.'

'You never told me that!' Rodolfo protested.

'I thought it might disturb you after your bad news at the university. Anyway, Dragos must have recognised your friend here when he attacked him, then raided the apartment when you were both out and taken his gun back.'

'Who's Dragos?' both men asked in unison.

'Oh, that's just my name for him. I thought he was a secret policeman.'

Vincenzo drained the last drops from his bottle.

'Anyway, the only thing for sure is that this Ugo business had nothing to do with me. I didn't even know the old fart. Was he really famous?'

'In some circles,' Rodolfo replied airily.

He was tempted to end Vincenzo's anxieties by confessing the truth, but that would start a crack in his relationship with Flavia that could never be made good. He decided to let Vincenzo sweat it out overnight and contact him in the morning. Besides, there was just the remotest possibility that he was telling the truth about the Curti killing. The pistol definitely existed, after all, and he had presumably concealed it in Rodolfo's room to throw suspicion on him if it were discovered in the course of a police search. No, he didn't owe Vincenzo any favours.

A gale of laughter swept over from the large table in the centre of the room.

'Who are these wankers?' yelled Vincenzo, whirling around. 'More happy fucks! Jesus, my luck's certainly run out tonight.'

'It's that young girl's birthday,' said Flavia. 'They're just having fun.'

'Fun? Fun? You think that's what life's about, having fun?'

'Then what?'

Vincenzo's lips crinkled in a contemptuous sneer.

'Stopping other people having fun,' he said. 'That's what it's all about, sweetheart.'

Flavia sniffed dismissively.

'Well, you're not going to stop us having fun. Is he, Rodolfo?

But Rodolfo did not seem inclined to answer. His eyes held Flavia's, and his gaze was deeply disturbed.

'. . . and add the garlic. Now the oil. No, not like that! In a slow drizzle, like the rain from heaven! Did your mother have to teach you to pee? How can anyone be so cack-handed? Listen to nature, only to nature! She always tells you what to do.'

Rather her than you, thought Rinaldi.

'Now a fine grating of nutmeg, like the winter snow dusting down from the mountains . . .'

'How much?'

Her lullaby-like reverie disturbed, the crone glared at him.

'How much what?'

'How much nutmeg!' screamed the chef.

She stared at him in apparently genuine amazement.

'*Ma quello che basta, stupido!*'

Just enough. Thanks, grandma.

'Enough, but not too much,' Rinaldi's mentor continued dreamily. 'For us it's traditional. How could a foreigner like you understand? Are you a Catholic or a Turk? Never mind, you're a man, that's the problem. Men should stay out of the kitchen. They don't have a clue about cooking. How can they, when they're not in tune with the rhythms of nature? We women have them in our bodies like the tides. Listen to nature, only to nature! Follow your innermost impulses and you can never go wrong!'

Romano Rinaldi just succeeded in resisting the temptation to follow this advice by swinging the frying pan round and beating the old bat to death with it, but it was touch and go. He knew that he wouldn't be able to hold out much longer. Somehow he finished the order and carried the dishes out to the serving counter two at a time. As he took the last one, the

211

now familiar howl erupted from his tormentor. The waiter duly appeared and arranged four of the plates on each arm, but the ninth defeated him.

'Bring that,' he ordered Rinaldi.

Lo Chef followed him out into the dining area, where the birthday celebrations were now in full swing. The waiter curtly directed Rinaldi to present the dish he was carrying to a girl of about sixteen who was sitting at the head of the table, a string of pearls which might or might not have been genuine about her neck, and a glow that certainly was on her face. The padded case in which the necklace had been presented lay open on the table.

Romano Rinaldi laid her pasta down with a flourish.

'It's your birthday, *signorina*?' he enquired.

The girl nodded. Rinaldi bowed deeply.

'*Tanti auguri.* May I ask your name?'

She shrugged awkwardly and blushed.

'*Mi chiamano Mimì, ma il mio nome è Lucia.*'

Romano Rinaldi touched her hand for the briefest of moments, then turned to the table in general and launched into the big tenor aria from the end of the first act of *La Bohème*, wittily changing Rodolfo's description of himself to 'Who am I? I'm a chef. What do I do? I cook.' This provoked much laughter and applause, but the real pleasure for Rinaldi was the realisation that his voice was perfectly adapted to the intimate acoustics of this space, and absolutely on key. In the studio he had to be miked up and his vocal interventions electronically tweaked in post-production to raise flat notes, lower sharp ones, and generally boost the volume, but now he didn't need any of those tricks. All that mattered here was pitch, range and style, and he had all three in spades.

As he forged forward, he realised with a certain pleased astonishment that he wasn't just imagining this in his usual drunken or stoned stupor. It was real, and everyone else in the room felt it. The entire company fell silent, transfixed by the narrative thrust of Puccini's melodic line and the naked glory of the human voice. Every eye was fixed on Rinaldi in respectful silence as he completed the entire aria with inexhaustible confidence, climaxing effortlessly on the difficult high 'La speranza!' which he held for fully ten seconds, bringing cries of 'Bravo!', before lowering his voice to a tender *pianissimo* for the concluding bars.

The result was a spontaneous and prolonged ovation from everyone in the restaurant. Standing there in his sauce-spattered apron, Rinaldi acknowledged his audience with appreciative bows, then turned to the overwhelmed birthday girl, kissed her hand lightly, and floated back towards the kitchen. As he passed the pizza oven, Normo stared at him in stunned silence. Rinaldi smiled casually and rounded the corner into the corridor, where he promptly slammed into some punk dropout with pink hair on his way back from the lavatory.

The youth, who was evidently drunk, ended up on the floor. When Rinaldi offered him a hand he received a torrent of obscene abuse in return, but just ignored it and walked on down the passageway. In that moment of exaltation, nothing could touch him. This was even better than *la coca*! Not only was he the star of the evening, but he'd just had a fabulous insight that would save his career from the disgrace of that disastrous cookery contest and propel it to still greater heights of glory and riches. *Real Work*: a new concept, a new show, a new book, a new . . .

Something hot, wet and sticky exploded on the wall beside him. The street kid he'd accidentally knocked over grabbed another of the plates of pizza that Normo had set out on the counter and hurled it at Rinaldi.

'*Stronzo di merda, vaffanculo!*'

'You're barred, you bastard!' screamed Normo ritualistical-ly, but he couldn't take any action, shut away as he was behind the counter. As for the two waiters, they seemed disinclined to enter the fray. The aggressor reached for another pizza. Rinaldi stepped smartly into the kitchen and dug the replica pistol out of the pocket of his jacket. Waiting until the third pizza and its plate exploded against the door to the lavatory, he stepped back into the corridor.

'Out,' he said decisively, waving the barrel of the pistol at the intruder.

The youth stared at the weapon with fascination rather than fear.

'Hey, that's my gun!'

'Out!' Rinaldi repeated, whirling the troublemaker around by his left arm and marching him towards the door.

'Remember what I said about us being left free to concentrate on public order issues?' Zen murmured to Bruno sarcastically.

He jerked his thumb back over his shoulder.

'Here's your chance to make the big arrest that brings promotion.'

The patrolman rolled his eyes.

'It's just one of those little *punkabestia* creeps who hang out under the portico of the Teatro Communale and in Piazza Verdi. We don't bother much with them. The drug dealers take care of the really violent ones. They don't want any trouble on their turf.'

'Neither, apparently, does *lo chef*,' Zen remarked as the troublemaker passed their table on his way to the front door, escorted by the foreign cook who was screaming 'Out! Out!' and prodding the younger man in the back with what was presumably some kitchen implement.

'Holy Christ!' said Bruno. 'That's Vincenzo Amadori.'

'What a charmer.'

'What do we do?'

Zen shrugged.

'No longer our case, is it?'

'Don't forget your stuff, Vincenzo!'

The cry came from the boyfriend of the young woman whom Zen had noticed earlier. He had grabbed the blue nylon duffle bag he had brought and was now squeezing through the tables towards the door.

'There could be evidence in that bag,' said Bruno urgently. 'We should take him!'

Zen lit a cigarette. Time to buy a new pack, he thought. The tobacconists would be closed by now, which just left the machines.

'Suit yourself,' he said. 'There'll be a lot of paperwork, you can say goodbye to the rest of your evening, and in the end the Carabinieri will get all the . . .'

But Bruno was already on his feet and gone. Ah, youth!

Out in the street, the situation had already changed. The short-order cook stumbled on the edge of the doorstep and the yob he was ejecting took advantage of this momentary loss of balance to turn on him. He emerged from the ensuing scuffle holding an automatic pistol. Aurelio Zen stubbed out his cigarette and called in on his work mobile to explain the situation and order the immediate dispatch of a squad car. Rising from the table, he collided with the young woman he had been eyeing earlier, who was now rushing towards the door with the skinnier of the two waiters in hot pursuit.

'And the bill?' he called plaintively. 'Over a hundred with the champagne!'

Zen followed the woman out to the street, where her companion had been grabbed and hoisted under the armpits by the *punkabestia* person, who was holding the pistol to the side of his head.

'Back off or the puppy gets it!' he yelled.

'Police!' Bruno retorted, keeping his distance and evidently uncertain what to do next. 'Lay down the gun! You're under arrest!'

The gunman didn't even glance at him, his attention entirely absorbed by the imposing spectacle of the young woman closing in on him.

'Put my boyfriend down this instant or you'll have me to deal with!' she shouted.

A patrol car swept around the corner, light bar pulsing but siren stilled, and screeched to a halt a few metres away. Vincenzo Amadori surveyed the situation, then lowered his weapon, released Rodolfo and burst into laughter.

'Ah, fuck!' he said.

Flavia took the pistol from his fingers and handed it to Bruno. Nobody else approached Vincenzo, who stood swaying about, alternately screwing up and widening his eyes like someone learning a potentially enthralling new skill.

'Are you a friend of his?' Zen asked Rodolfo.

'Who are you?'

'A police officer.'

'We share an apartment.'

'What's in the bag?'

'Just some clothes he asked me to bring him.'

While Bruno, aided by his fellow patrolmen, handcuffed Amadori, Zen started looking through the contents of the duffle bag. He lifted out a striped cream silk shirt bearing the Versace label and held it up to the light of the restaurant's neon sign. Several brown stains were visible on the right-hand chest panel.

Zen called Bruno over.

'It looks like you may have been right about there being evidence in the bag.'

Bruno peered at the shirt, unimpressed.

'A couple of wine stains?'

'Let's see what the DNA tests say. But if it's blood rather than wine, as I have reason to suppose, then we'll have stolen both the Curti and Ugo cases back from the Carabinieri, and you'll be a sergeant next month.'

Tony Speranza woke up feeling like hell. Actually, he woke up feeling like hell every morning, but as he could never remember much about the day before, still less the days before that, this always came as a surprise.

He shuddered out of bed and padded through to the kitchen, where he cracked a bottle of Budweiser before proceeding to the living room and unmuting the TV, which had been on all night. A post-breakfast talk show for bored housewives was in progress, some hermetically groomed babe in a power suit. When Tony's eyes finally focused, he saw that a title in the corner of the screen identified her as Delia Anselmi, personal assistant to the famous star branded as *Lo Chef Che Canta e Incanta*.

'Romano's new concept is just awesome,' she was gushing. 'To think that he's actually been working in disguise at an ordinary neighbourhood *trattoria*, doing research for this fabulous new series. Returning to his roots, as he put it to me last night, Stella. And I want you to know that he was weeping!'

The buxom, genetically modified presenter beamed.

'That's just great, Delia! I want you both to know that we're all weeping too, but we're weeping tears of joy.'

'Thanks for sharing, Stella! I'm really moved, and I just know that Romano will be too. I can't of course disclose the location of the restaurant where Romano decided to go "back to the rock face", as he put it to me. That would compromise the integrity and authenticity of the whole experience, but it's also for legal reasons following Romano's heroic and decisive intervention in the dramatic arrest of Lorenzo Curti's assassin last night. But we will shortly be filming him there, fly-on-the-wall style, and the resulting series, *Real Work*, will be shown . . .'

'. . . exclusively on this channel,' the presenter put in.

'. . . early in the autumn. I just know that this is a break-through concept that is going to entirely change the whole way we look at . . .'

Tony Speranza hit the mute button and shambled over to his phone. No messages from the Amadori family, despite the turn of the screw he had administered the day before by call-ing the Questura and shopping Vincenzo as Edgardo Ugo's attacker. Of course, they might not have been told yet. The police were so inefficient. He returned to the kitchen, swapped the Bud for a Jack Daniels and then shambled back to collapse in front of the TV, surfing to a twenty-four-hour news channel which was showing footage of some botoxed presenter heavy-lipping a huge microphone as if it were a phallus. 'Supercop from Rome Cracks Curti Case' read the title. Tony's hand dart-ed for the remote control.

'. . . can confirm that Vincenzo Amadori is in custody. He will face charges later today in regard to the murder of Lorenzo Curti and also the shooting of Professor Edgardo Ugo. Forensic tests indicate that the weapon used in both crimes is that which was in possession of the accused at the time of his arrest late last night by a crack team of Polizia di Stato operatives under the leadership of Vice-Questore Aurelio Zen. At a news confer-ence earlier this morning, Dottor Zen and the officer in charge of the investigation, Commissario Salvatore Brunetti, stated that . . .'

He pushed the mute button again and glumly watched footage of two men, one in police uniform, the other in a suit and overcoat, addressing a group of journalists. Fuck, he thought. Fuck fuck fuck fuck fuck. So much for his pension plan.

Then he had an idea.

It was about eleven o'clock when Tony Speranza arrived at the Questura. A blanket of cold, hard smog enveloped the entire city. Tony was wearing a powder-blue suit with a dark blue shirt and tie and black brogues. He was neat, clean, shaved and relatively sober, and didn't care who knew it. He was everything the well-dressed private detective ought to be. He was calling for one million euros.

Tony stated his business to the sergeant at the desk, who asked him to wait and then made a number of whispered phone calls. About five minutes later, two armed officers in uniform approached the desk.

The sergeant said tonelessly, 'Commissario Brunetti will see you now, Signor Speranza.'

The two officers escorted him up the wide staircase to the first floor. Neither spoke nor looked at him, but he was pleased – proud, even – of their presence. It proved that he was finally being taken seriously, with the respect that he deserved.

Having traversed a lateral corridor, he was ushered into a large office. There were two men present. Tony recognised them as the pair he had seen earlier on the TV news report. Better and better! He was going straight to the top!

The shorter of the men looked at him, but did not invite him to sit down.

'We understand that you have come to claim the reward offered by the Curti family for information leading to the arrest of the killer,' he said.

'Correct.'

'As it happens, the person we believe to be the killer is already under arrest. On what basis are you therefore claiming the reward?'

Tony had rehearsed this scene many times on the way in and had his answer ready.

'Your case against Vincenzo Amadori rests on the fact that at the time of his arrest he was holding the gun used to shoot not only Curti but also Professor Edgardo Ugo. That is merely circumstantial evidence. I, on the other hand, have definitive proof that Amadori was indeed in the place and at the time that Ugo was shot. On the basis of the information that I possess, there can be no doubt that he will be convicted of that crime. But since the same weapon was used in both incidents, and was in his possession, it follows that he must have shot Curti too. It will be an open and shut case.'

The taller man now spoke.

'Just what is the nature of this information, Signor Speranza?'

Tony laughed lightly to indicate that he hadn't been born yesterday.

'I would naturally only be prepared to disclose its full extent once the payment of the reward has been agreed by the Curti family. But I can reveal that it involves electronic surveillance techniques with a logged computer record and will stand up in court.'

He smiled at the two officials.

'We're talking the information age equivalent of blood on the hands.'

The taller man glanced at the uniformed officers, who had remained in the room, one to either side of Speranza.

'All right,' he sighed. 'Take him down to the cellars and sweat it out of him. The works, okay? I want every detail by three at the latest. Including the stuff he's forgotten he knew.'

The uniforms moved in and grasped Speranza by either arm in the manner known to pulp fiction as 'vice-like'. It did indeed feel very vicious.

'But . . . but . . . but . . .' Tony spluttered.

The official smiled enigmatically.

'The criminal always makes one fatal mistake,' he said. 'You came here demanding a reward on the basis of having proof that the person who murdered Lorenzo Curti also shot Edgardo Ugo with the same gun.'

'But it's true!'

The other man nodded.

'It's certainly true. What you overlooked, however, is that it's your gun.'

Tony looked at him in complete bewilderment.

'Mine? But how can you know that?'

'Ah, that might well have taken some considerable time. The weapon had almost certainly been acquired on the black market, and was not officially registered. Fortunately, however, we were in possession of a clue that eventually led us, after a sleepless night and much profound cogitation that tested our professional skills as never before, to the irrefutable truth.'

Tony laughed bravely.

'You're bluffing! What clue?'

'Your name is engraved on the barrel, *signore*,' said Aurelio Zen.